The Story of Painting

This sea scene eventually gave its name to a whole art movement. You can see the full painting on page 62.

Real gold was used to decorate this medieval feast scene. Find out more on page 25.

The Story of Painting

Abigail Wheatley

Designed by Zöe Wray

Illustrated by
Uwe Mayer and Ian McNee

Consultant: Dr. Erika Langmuir, OBE

Contents

This portrait of a Roman couple has survived almost untouched for around 2,000 years. The full painting is shown on page 14.

Cave Painting
to
Classical

People started painting pictures tens of thousands of years ago – even before they began writing or building houses. Many ancient people believed that pictures had mysterious, magical powers, and created them as part of their religion. Some paintings have survived for an astonishingly long time, starting with the first cave paintings, made around 30,000 years ago.

An ancient town-dweller,
decorating his home

From
30,000
years ago

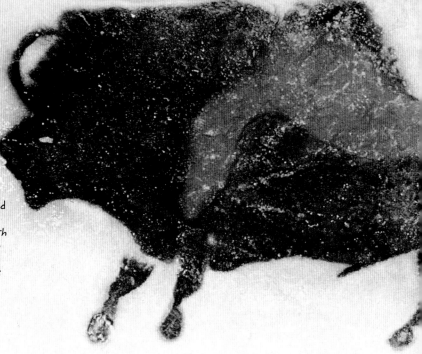

Early cave painters drew with coloured rocks ground into powder. Sometimes they mixed the powder with animal fat or plant sap to make paint. Powder used like this to colour paint is called "pigment".

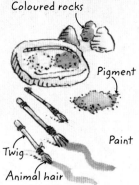

Coloured rocks

Pigment

Paint

Twig

Animal hair

They made simple paint brushes, and scratched lines with sticks and stones.

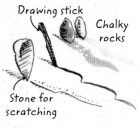

Drawing stick

Chalky rocks

Stone for scratching

To see in dark caves, they burned animal fat in stone lamps.

Fat

Plant fibre wick

The first painters

No one really knows where or when the story of painting began. People started making marks and drawings thousands and thousands of years ago – so long ago that time and weather have worn away almost all the traces. But, deep inside caves, and on sheltered rocks, people are still discovering incredibly ancient paintings that look almost as new as the day they were made.

About 30,000 years ago, deep in dark and mysterious caves, by the light of flickering stone lamps, early people started to draw. Their lines followed the natural bulges and creases in the cave walls to pick out the shapes of ancient animals – from lumbering mammoths to fierce cave bears. They filled in some of

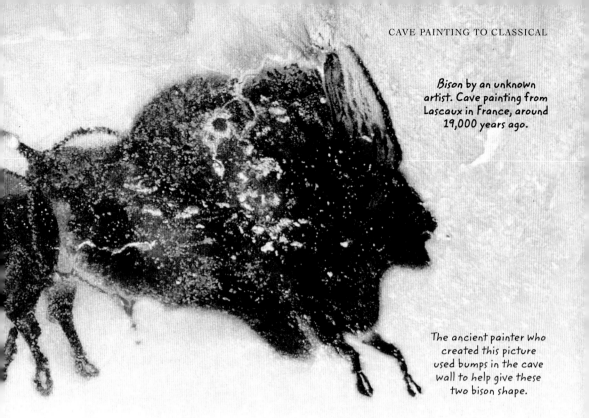

Bison by an unknown artist. Cave painting from Lascaux in France, around 19,000 years ago.

The ancient painter who created this picture used bumps in the cave wall to help give these two bison shape.

the animal shapes, so they looked more solid; they drew others that overlapped, to look like herds on the move. The people who made these cave paintings lived by hunting animals for food and clothing. So maybe the pictures were a kind of hunting magic, to try to make sure the hunt went well.

Making marks

All kinds of ancient pictures – from complex scenes to simple scratched lines – have been found in caves and on rocks all around the world. No one is sure exactly why they were made, but the ancient artists must have felt they were very important, as they put a lot of effort into them.

Blowing paint

Hand-shaped gap

Many ancient painters made hand outlines, by blowing mouthfuls of paint over and around their hands.

Plastering the wall

Paintings

Bull's skull

Hand prints

Paints

Early town-dwellers of Çatalhöyük painted their house walls, perhaps as part of family burial ceremonies.

The first wall paintings

From **8,000** years ago

Around 8,000 years ago, people first began to build mud brick houses and towns – and to decorate them with paintings. At Çatalhöyük, an early town in Turkey, people covered their walls with red and black patterns and pictures of people and animals. But mud brick was rather lumpy, so they spread a smooth, white paste, called plaster, onto their walls; when it was dry, they painted on top. This method worked so well that soon everyone was using it.

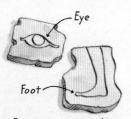

Eye

Foot

Egyptian painters always drew eyes front-on, but showed feet sideways – as you can see in the painting opposite.

Egyptian art

From around 5,000 years ago, the ancient Egyptians were creating their own sophisticated and colourful pictures of awesome gods and rulers, dramatic battles and detailed scenes of family life. Egyptian painters followed strict rules: for example, they always showed things from the angle that was easiest to recognize. So heads, legs and arms were shown from the side, while chests were shown from the front.

Grid

They drew people on a measured grid, so they were all a similar shape.

From design to painting

The walls of grand Egyptian tombs, temples and palaces echoed with the sounds of busy craftsmen – wall painting was very much a team effort. First, a supervisor drew up the designs on a wooden board painted white; then one worker smoothed plaster onto the walls, one marked out the design with black outlines and another painted on the colours.

The Egyptians believed that their pictures had amazing powers. Tomb paintings were designed to help the soul of the dead person to pass safely to the afterlife – a magical place where the dead were supposed to live happily forever.

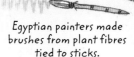

Egyptian painters made brushes from plant fibres tied to sticks.

Colourful rocks

They ground up naturally colourful rocks to make different pigments...

...and mixed them with glue to make paint.

This wall painting is from the tomb of a man named Nebamun. It shows him with his family in the afterlife.

Nebamun is enjoying a popular Egyptian pastime – hunting birds – with his wife, his young son and his pet cat.

Both Nebamun's hands have the knuckles showing. It may look as if he has two left hands, but the Egyptians always showed hands like this.

Hunting in the marshes by an unknown artist. Wall painting from Thebes in Egypt, around 3,350 years ago.

Ladies in blue by an unknown artist. Fresco from Crete in Greece, around 3,500 years ago.

This wall painting by a Minoan artist from Crete shows women dressed for a religious ceremony.

Plaster

Minoan painters mixed fine, white plaster into a paste...

...smoothed it on to the wall...

Wet plaster

...and painted their designs quickly, before the plaster dried.

Paint soaking in

Painting in ancient Greece

The ancient Egyptians were great seafarers, and passed on their skills and ideas – including painting – to people all around the Mediterranean sea. By around 4,000 years ago, the Minoan people, who lived on the island of Crete and in other parts of Greece, were decorating their houses and palaces with wall paintings of people, flowers and animals. Their paintings were a bit like Egyptian ones – but with some crucial differences.

The Minoans discovered that, if they painted onto walls when the plaster was still wet, their colours soaked right in, and didn't flake off the surface of the plaster over time. This technique, known as "fresco", became one of the most popular painting methods for the next 3,000 years, and it's still used today.

The Minoans also broke some of the rigid Egyptian rules about how to draw things. They started showing people and animals from different angles, and painted their figures without using a grid, so their pictures had a more natural, flowing feel.

From **2,500** years ago

Classical style

By 2,500 years ago, ancient Greece was producing some of the greatest ever painters, sculptors, writers, scientists and philosophers. This time of amazing creativity was known as the classical period. Painting was a vital part of classical Greek culture and there were regular painting competitions, so artists could show off their latest tricks. The Greeks painted everything from majestic gods and heroes to portraits of living people. Their paintings were very lifelike, but they liked to improve on real life too, to make things look more beautiful than they really were.

Sadly, most large-scale paintings from classical Greece have been lost over the centuries. So we have to imagine what they were like by studying painted decorations on Greek vases, reading ancient writings and looking at copies of Greek paintings made by the next keen artists who came along – the Romans.

This building is a Greek temple.

Sculptures being covered in paint

The ancient Greeks used waterproof paints to decorate the outsides of buildings. Find out more on the next page.

From
2,000
years ago

Roman art

For centuries, the Greeks were seen as the creative geniuses of the ancient world. Even when their magnificent civilization was taken over by the warlike Romans around 2,000 years ago, Greek skills and ideas were still in great demand. The Romans, who were based in Italy, conquered most of Europe and parts of Africa and Asia. They were proud of their vast empire, but they were also huge admirers of Greek culture.

This wall painting is a portrait of a Roman husband and wife who lived in the town of Pompeii, in Italy.

The faces look as if they are carefully drawn from real life — you can even see the worry lines on the man's forehead.

Portrait of Terentius Neo and his wife by an unknown artist. Fresco from Pompeii in Italy, around the year 50.

Roman artists often copied Greek pictures and hired Greek painters to work for them. But, unlike the Greeks, who made their paintings more beautiful than real life, the Romans liked to paint things just as they were – lumps, bumps, wrinkles and all. Many of their portraits are so lifelike, they make you feel you are meeting real ancient Romans face to face.

Pretend view

The Romans painted lifelike landscapes on the walls of their town houses, to give an illusion of space.

Paints and pigments

Both the ancient Greeks and Romans relied a lot on the fresco technique developed by the Minoans. But they also painted on wooden panels using ground-up colours, or "pigments", mixed with egg. This made a quick-drying paint known as egg tempera. For painting pictures on the outsides of buildings, or on ships, they dissolved pigments in hot wax, to make encaustic – a long-lasting, waterproof paint.

Rocks containing lead

Chalk

Iron ore

The Greeks and Romans made pigments from rocks and some metals...

Ground pigment

Egg

Wooden panel

...mixed them with egg for paint that dried fast...

Early Christians

The Romans believed in – and painted – many gods and goddesses, but, at the height of their power, a new religion began to spread through the Roman empire. It was called Christianity. The Roman authorities banned it, so Christians met secretly in underground tombs and rooms. On the walls, they painted scenes from religious writings such as the Bible, showing Jesus Christ, his life and his followers. When the Roman empire fell apart, around 1,500 years ago, it was the Christians who kept up the painting skills they had learned from the Romans.

Beeswax

...or mixed them with hot wax to make waterproof paint.

This delicate medieval painting shows an angel with feathery wings, set against a background of real gold. The full painting is shown on page 22.

The Middle Ages

The end of the Roman empire meant the start of difficult times in Europe, as rival leaders battled fiercely for land and power. The constant fighting disrupted life so badly that most people had no time for art and culture. But, here and there, some Christians kept on painting, and as things gradually began to settle down, this Christian art spread. This time of conflict and change is called the Middle Ages, and its people, art and culture are known as "medieval".

Imaginary monsters like this were often used to decorate medieval paintings.

From
the year
476

Byzantine painting

In the 5th century, ferocious horseback warriors galloped into Italy from northern and eastern Europe and in the year 476 they overthrew the last Roman emperor. In the West, the mighty Roman empire came to a dramatic end. Wars raged, as warlords competed to carve out their own territories, and peaceful activities like painting were largely forgotten.

This Byzantine painting shows Jesus as a baby with his mother, Mary.

Byzantine painters wanted their pictures to look dignified and holy, rather than lifelike. You can see that these figures and their robes have been simplified, to make the shapes more elegant.

A real gold background and highlights give the painting a rich glow. For the Byzantines, gold was a way of showing the pure light of heaven.

The Mother of God of Tenderness by an unknown artist. Egg tempera paint on wood, Byzantine, around 1131.

But in Byzantium (the eastern part of the empire, which covered what is now Greece, Turkey and the Middle East), life was relatively calm. Byzantium had its own Christian emperor, who ruled from the city of Constantinople (now Istanbul). Byzantine painters made Christian pictures, using the same techniques and materials as the Romans: painting wooden panels with egg tempera or wax-based encaustic paints.

The Byzantines thought their paintings were very holy – they even believed that some of their pictures had been sent to Earth by God. Painters copied these images again and again, and stuck gold on them, to show how precious they were. These paintings are known as icons, Greek for "images".

The image-smashers

In 730, the Byzantine emperor started worrying that people were becoming too fond of icons, and not thinking enough about the holy people the icons showed. So he sent out men, known as iconoclasts, or "image-smashers", to destroy them. There were dreadful scenes, as the iconoclasts rushed into churches, past protesting crowds, and tore paintings down, or splashed white paint over them.

But, a hundred years later, Byzantine officials decided icons should be allowed again. Artists in Greece, Eastern Europe and Russia still paint icons today.

The Byzantine iconoclasts, or image-smashers, were so good at their job that very few paintings survived.

Byzantine painters used real gold, known as gold leaf. It came in sheets, kept in animal skin booklets.

Protective booklet

Sheet of gold leaf

To stick it on, they first painted on watery clay as a glue...

Clay

...then stuck down strips of gold...

...smoothed them with a soft brush...

...and scraped off any excess gold with a knife.

White paint

Smashing icons

From
the year
600

Painting and praying

While painting was flourishing in Byzantium, it was disappearing in the West. Constant wars disrupted life for everyone: families were divided and crops were ruined. People were so busy just surviving, they had no time for things like reading, writing and painting.

But painting never quite died out thanks to Christian monks, who lived together in monasteries away from other people, and led religious lives. Although they were sometimes disturbed by local wars, they tried to keep to a strict regime of prayer and study – and painting.

Old book
for copying

Newly
copied page

Monks sat for hours each day copying out old books, and painting richly coloured illustrations.

Sometimes, monks made their books more interesting by adding comments in the margins, or painting imaginary monsters like this.

Making manuscripts

Monks' lives revolved around religious writings, such as the Bible, and most monasteries had great libraries, full of religious books of many different types, shapes and sizes. But, in those days, printing hadn't been invented, so monks had to make their own books, copying out all the words and pictures by hand.

It could take months or even years to copy out just one book, and fill it with intricate illustrations, picked out in bright, jewel-like colours and gold leaf. Plenty of light was needed for this fine work, but window glass was expensive. So, on cold days the wind whistled through the great empty window frames, and the poor monks shivered at their copying desks.

St. Luke by an unknown artist. Egg tempera paint on animal skin, Western European, around 800.

A monk painted this picture for a handmade, elaborately illustrated book — or illuminated manuscript.

The man is St. Luke. His chair isn't very realistic, but it's big and luxurious to make him look important.

The winged bull isn't supposed to be a real animal — it's St. Luke's symbol. You can find out more about saints' symbols on the next page.

Monks mixed pigments with egg to make egg tempera paint.

They painted onto sheets of smoothed animal skin and added gold leaf...

...then they stitched the sheets together into a book.

Monks adapted the painting methods used by the Romans, but their style was very different. For them, the religious message was the vital thing, so they didn't worry about making their paintings too lifelike. They used egg tempera paints on pages made from treated animal skin. Their handmade books are known as manuscripts, and the pictures in them are called illuminations, because they are so bright.

From
1000

Teaching the faithful

Gradually, as the years passed, life began to settle down, even outside the monasteries. Powerful kings ruled wealthy kingdoms, with bands of knights in gleaming metal armour to help them keep order. Wars still broke out regularly, as neighbouring rulers squabbled, but most ordinary medieval people went about their daily business in peace. Some even had time for reading, writing and painting again.

The Annunciation with St. Ansano and St. Margaret by Simone Martini. Egg tempera paint on wood, Italian, 1333.

This painting was made for a church. The central scene shows the angel Gabriel giving a message to Jesus' mother, Mary. The side panels show St. Margaret (right) and St. Ansano (left).

Everyone had more time for religion, too. By now, Christian churches were springing up in every town and village, so monks and priests could educate ordinary people about the Bible. But, as most people still couldn't read or write, books were no good to them. Instead, religious teachers relied on paintings to get their message across. They paid artists to paint pictures of Christian stories all over their churches – on the walls and ceilings, on wooden panels and even on the window glass.

Halo

Saint

Painters showed a bright glow, or halo, around the heads of angels and holy people, such as saints.

These paintings were easy to recognize because, just like the monks copying out their manuscripts, medieval painters copied from other pictures. This meant that everyone painted particular things in the same way. For example, painters always gave angels feathery wings. You can see this in the painting opposite, and in the column on the right are some other things you might spot in medieval pictures.

Anyone holding a palm leaf was a martyr – someone who died for their beliefs. Can you spot two palms in the side panels of the painting opposite?

Painting for profit

Paintings were not only useful for teaching – they were beautiful, too, with their bright colours and rich details, real gold highlights and graceful, curving shapes. Soon, everyone wanted them. Kings and queens, noblemen and women and wealthy merchants all paid good money for paintings to adorn their palaces and castles, or to decorate their local churches. Many rich people could read now, so they began to buy luxury books with lavish illustrations. Painting had become big business.

Some saints and martyrs had special objects, or symbols. St. Peter held keys, because he was thought to have the keys of heaven.

Heavenly glow

A dove was supposed to represent the holy spirit.

Crushing pigments

Mixing paint

Master painter

Carving a panel

A medieval painter's workshop like this one was a bustling place, full of assistants preparing pigments, paints, brushes and panels.

The painter's workshop

With rich people prepared to pay handsomely for paintings, it wasn't long before painters began setting up workshops all over the place. Successful artists had long queues of rich clients – known as patrons – and more work than they could manage on their own. So they hired assistants to help them.

Painters' assistants usually started out as teenagers, and spent years learning all the necessary skills. They worked from dawn till dusk, while there was light to see by, doing all the chores around the workshop. They prepared wooden panels and ruled lines on pages, ready for painting to begin. Then they ground pigments and mixed them with egg to make paint.

As assistants learned more, some were trusted to do a bit of drawing and painting, too – provided they took care to copy their master's style exactly. This wasn't to trick anyone into thinking the master had done all the work – it was just so that different parts of the painting would match each other.

January by the Limbourg brothers: Pol, Herman and Jean. Egg tempera paint on animal skin, Netherlandish, 1413-16.

The painting is from a prayer book made for the Duke of Berry, a French nobleman. Part of the book is a calendar, and this scene illustrates January.

It's a picture of a winter feast hosted by the duke. He is the one sitting at the table in the fur hat and the bright blue robe.

The figures in grey floppy hats at the left of the painting may be self-portraits of two of the brothers who painted the scene.

The bright blue in this painting comes from lapis lazuli, a semi-precious stone. It was imported all the way from Afghanistan, and was worth even more than gold.

Picky patrons

Patrons could be very fussy. They asked for all kinds of paintings, from Bible scenes and famous love stories to dashing pictures of King Arthur and his knights. Some paid for luxury materials, such as gold leaf and paints made from precious stones, to show off their wealth, or even asked for their portraits to be included in the painting, so everyone would know who had paid for it.

Crushed lapis lazuli

Expensive blue paint

25

From
1300

Painting goes international

Medieval painting started off as a local affair. Each master painter trained up a bunch of assistants, and eventually they set up their own businesses nearby. Clusters of workshops grew up, all producing art in one distinctive style – manuscripts decorated with a special type of pattern, say, or paintings with a specific style of figures.

But, as time went by, kings and queens, nobles and wealthy merchants began to travel widely, all over Europe, and they saw different painting styles wherever they went. It wasn't long before they began to invite foreign painters to come back and work for them at home. Not to be outdone, local painters were quick to pick up new styles, and adapt them to their own work. Painting was fast becoming a truly international business.

On the road

Soon it became normal for artists and craftworkers of all kinds – from painters and poets to metalworkers and stonemasons – to travel around for a few years as part of their training. They took work in as many different places as they could, learning new techniques and styles, and passing on their own skills wherever they went. Travelling painters often carried paper and ink with them, so they could copy down any useful designs they saw, or sketch the different animals, plants and inspiring landscapes they came across on their journeys.

Famous painting

Essential painting kit

Young painters sometimes journeyed far to see famous works of art. They called the time they spent learning and travelling their "wanderyears".

Mix and match

Making notes and sketches encouraged artists to look around them for inspiration when they got home, too. They began to make detailed drawings from nature, and combined these with ideas and designs from their travels. With all this mixing up and sharing, artists no longer had to rely on copying directly from their masters, so local painting styles slowly began to disappear. Most medieval painters still liked to simplify shapes and use brilliant, glowing colours, to make their designs more striking and vivid than real life. But even this was about to change...

Metalpoint   Sketch

Watercolour

By now, artists were sketching on paper, using a kind of pencil known as metalpoint, and watercolour paints made of pigments mixed with water.

These jay birds are from a sketchbook kept by the Italian painter Pisanello. He sketched many animals and plants to use in his paintings.

Bird studies by Antonio Pisano (known as Pisanello). Watercolour paint on paper, Italian, before 1455.

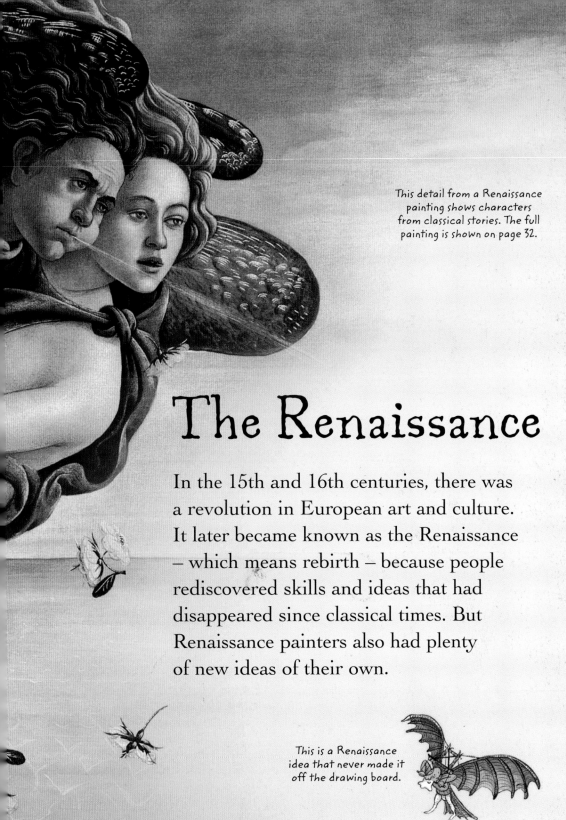

This detail from a Renaissance painting shows characters from classical stories. The full painting is shown on page 32.

The Renaissance

In the 15th and 16th centuries, there was a revolution in European art and culture. It later became known as the Renaissance – which means rebirth – because people rediscovered skills and ideas that had disappeared since classical times. But Renaissance painters also had plenty of new ideas of their own.

This is a Renaissance idea that never made it off the drawing board.

From
1400

New paints and techniques

One of the greatest inventions of the Renaissance was an entirely new method of painting. Since classical times artists had used quick-drying egg tempera, which meant they had to plan their paintings very carefully, working on one small patch at a time, before the paint dried. But, in the Netherlands, sometime in the 15th century, painters started mixing their pigments with oil instead.

The result was oil paint. It dried slowly, which meant painters could now make changes and improvements to the picture as they went along. They could also paint it on in thin coats they could almost see through, building up layers to create realistic textures and lifelike light effects.

Family talent

The new paints caught on fast. Soon one family of painters from the Netherlands, the van Eycks, shot to fame, astonishing everyone with their amazingly lifelike oil paintings, filled with texture and soft light.

Hubert, Jan and Margaret van Eyck, two brothers and a sister from the Netherlands, produced such amazing oil paintings, some people even thought they had invented the new paint.

Jan van Eyck (in his best hat)

Fashionable patron

The Arnolfini Portrait
by Jan van Eyck.
Oil paint on wood,
Netherlandish, 1434.

This painting shows a
wealthy couple in their
comfortable home in
the Netherlands.

The artist, Jan van Eyck,
proudly signed his name
just above the round
mirror on the back wall.
Before this time, many
painters didn't sign their
work, so we don't know
their names.

The man in the painting is
thought to be Giovanni
Arnolfini, a rich Italian
merchant. The luxurious
furnishings show his
wealth, but also let van
Eyck show off his skill at
painting textures.

Oil

Pigment

Oil paint

To make their oil paints,
painters used plant oils
such as linseed oil (from
flax seeds) and walnut oil.

Everything in this portrait by Jan van Eyck looks
incredibly real – as if each object was copied carefully
from real life. Light seems to glow through the
window, the fabrics look soft and warm, and each
fluffy hair on the little dog has been lovingly recorded.
The man and woman look like real people, too. This
type of effect was so new and exciting that artists all
across Europe were soon using oil paints, too.

Walnuts

Flax

From
1450

Classical influences

Meanwhile, in Italy, painters were becoming just as excited about their own discoveries. But these weren't new inventions – they were ancient remains.

The ancient Romans had lived in Italy centuries before, so there were Roman ruins, coins and statues scattered all over the place. Many Italians took these things for granted, but by the late 15th century, there was a sudden craze for anything and everything to do with ancient Rome and Greece. No classical paintings had been found by then, but Italian painters started studying Greek and Roman writings, and sketching all the ancient statues they could get their hands on.

The Renaissance scene below shows Venus, the Roman goddess of love, being born from the ocean waves and blown to shore by the two figures on the left.

The painter, Botticelli, followed classical writings for most of the details, but he also added some puzzles – it's not known just who the figure on the right is supposed to be.

The Birth of Venus by Sandro Botticelli. Egg tempera paint on canvas, Italian, around 1485.

Classical nude

Roman emperor

Wealthy art lover

Renaissance artists

Soon, they were creating their own pictures of the classical myths, gods and heroes they had read about in books, and painting in a very lifelike style that was inspired by Roman sculptures.

The classical craze

Of course, classical scenes weren't Christian, so they weren't suitable for churches or chapels. And, as many artists copied from naked, or "nude", classical statues, a lot of ordinary people found the paintings shocking. Luckily for the painters, though, some rich Italians had become just as fascinated by all things classical. The city of Florence, in particular, was full of art lovers keen to explore new ideas and invest in the latest art. Florence's wealthiest family, the Medici, bought heaps of paintings with classical themes and helped to spread the new fashion.

To add to the excitement, some artists decided to start mixing together different classical scenes, and adding extra details with hidden meanings, as puzzles for their patrons. Only well-educated people, who had read all about classical myths and heroes, could understand what these paintings were about – so more and more people wanted one, to show how clever they were.

By the 16th century, the classical craze had spread all over Europe, and paintings of Greek and Roman stories were everywhere. But even more popular was the lifelike style inspired by the classical statues.

Lorenzo de Medici, a wealthy banker from Florence, displayed Roman statues in his garden, and encouraged artists to draw them.

Tricks of the eye

Mirror

Brunelleschi discovered how perspective worked by painting onto a mirror, tracing over the reflection of a famous building.

As Italian painters became more and more interested in creating lifelike paintings, they started searching for new, more convincing ways of creating the illusion of depth, too. Around 1413, a Florentine architect called Filippo Brunelleschi discovered "perspective" – a foolproof method of marking out space in a very convincing way, so that paintings looked like real spaces instead of flat surfaces. It was such an exciting breakthrough, everyone wanted to try it. One of the keenest was Florentine painter Paolo Uccello, who spent sleepless nights perfecting the technique.

The rules of perspective

To create perspective, the artist draws a line across the painting at the level of the viewer's eyes.

The eyelevel line marks out the horizon, where the ground and the sky seem to meet.

The vanishing point is the spot where parallel lines appear to merge in the distance.

Faraway things look very small.

Eye level

Nearby things look large.

This river runs towards the vanishing point, almost at eye level.

In this painting, the artist, Uccello, has arranged the scene to lead viewers' eyes towards the vanishing point.

Many of the horses, dogs and hunters are looking at, or moving towards, the vanishing point.

Hunt in the Forest by Paolo Uccello. Oil paint on wood, Italian, around 1436.

Mixing paints

Sketching from classical statues

Stretching canvas

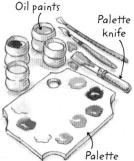

In a busy Renaissance workshop, there was plenty to do for assistants, even if they weren't allowed to do any actual painting.

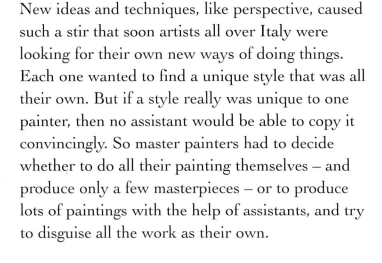

Oil paints

Palette knife

Palette

The most trusted assistant laid out paints for the master painter on a board called a palette.

Painters go solo

New ideas and techniques, like perspective, caused such a stir that soon artists all over Italy were looking for their own new ways of doing things. Each one wanted to find a unique style that was all their own. But if a style really was unique to one painter, then no assistant would be able to copy it convincingly. So master painters had to decide whether to do all their painting themselves – and produce only a few masterpieces – or to produce lots of paintings with the help of assistants, and try to disguise all the work as their own.

Helping out

There were still plenty of chores for assistants to do. They ground pigments, mixed paints and prepared surfaces for painting. Many painters were now using strong canvas cloths stretched flat on wooden frames.

These were much lighter and easier to construct than big wooden panels.

In some workshops, master painters still handed their designs and sketches to assistants and allowed them to start the painting, before finishing off the fine details themselves. But other masters refused to allow assistants near their paintings. It was around this time that most painters started signing their names on their paintings, so everyone would know who had painted them.

The successful painter Raphael drew this head of a baby angel. As he became more famous, he gave sketches like this to his assistants, to turn into paintings.

Artistic rivalry

The art world quickly became fraught with rivalry and suspicion. Some artists forged the signatures of famous painters, or tried to steal their latest designs. Others became suspicious of their assistants, in case they were hired as spies by rivals. They guarded their unfinished pictures carefully, locked up their sketchbooks and painted their most important works in secret.

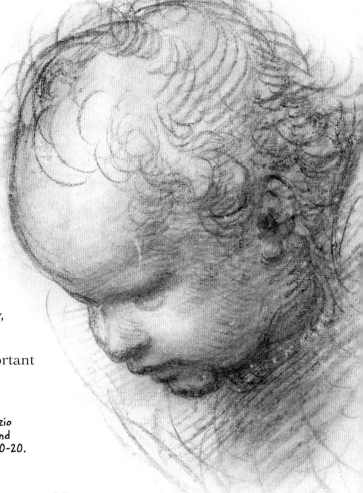

Head of a Cherub by Raffaello Sanzio (known as Raphael). Black chalk and charcoal on paper, Italian, around 1500-20.

The Holy Family by Michelangelo Buonarroti. Oil paint on wood, Italian, about 1504-5.

Baby Jesus is shown here with Mary and Joseph in a landscape with classical-style nude figures.

Florentine artist Michelangelo studied real people before painting these figures, to help him make their muscles and movements look more convincing.

The natural look

From
1500

Although Renaissance painters were all looking for their own unique style, they agreed that lifelike painting was the way forward. With the help of perspective and oil painting techniques for capturing light and textures, things had come a long way already.

But many painters felt they needed to work harder to create natural-looking landscapes and human figures. So they began to make special studies of real trees, rocks and landscapes to use in their paintings. Florentine artist Leonardo da Vinci even invented a new perspective technique especially for landscapes. He found that strong, red-brown shades made some things seem close, while faded, blueish tints made others look far away. This technique, known as aerial perspective, remained popular for hundreds of years.

Some Renaissance painters even made drawings of dead bodies, to help them understand muscles and bones, and paint human figures more realistically.

Real people

Of course, painters wanted the people in their paintings to look just as natural as the landscape settings. Copying from lifelike ancient statues was some help, but painters soon started making drawings of real people. For classical-style nudes, this meant drawing from naked models. Some people found this shocking, but it was definitely the best way to get a lifelike result.

As well as painting more natural-looking bodies, painters also began to create more lifelike faces. This was especially useful for making portraits of living people. Rich patrons were soon lining up to have their features preserved forever in a work of art. Some artists even made a living almost entirely from painting portraits. The people in Renaissance portraits are long dead, so there's no way of telling how accurate the pictures were – but it often does feel as though a real person is gazing out at you.

King Henry VIII of England asked German painter Holbein to paint lifelike portraits of several women, to see which one was pretty enough for him to marry.

Multi-tasking

Some of the greatest Renaissance painters weren't just good with a brush. From an amazingly early age, Leonardo da Vinci astonished everyone with his artistic gifts, but he also became famous for his other talents. He came up with designs for amazing new inventions, from flying machines to mechanical weapons, and he studied science and nature, too.

Leather and wood wings

Handles for flapping

Leonardo da Vinci, a man of many talents, invented several amazing flying machines, including one based on birds' wings — though he never managed to make it work.

This is Leonardo da Vinci's most famous painting. It's a portrait of a mysterious woman — no one is quite sure who she was, or whether she's smiling or not.

Some experts think the woman in the painting may have been a merchant's wife named Lisa.

Leonardo hid the corners of her eyes and mouth in shadow, so her smile became blurred. That's why she looks serious as well as smiling.

Mona Lisa by Leonardo da Vinci. Oil paint on wood, Italian, 1503-6.

Michelangelo's masterpiece

Michelangelo's lunch

But Leonardo wasn't the only Renaissance artist with many different skills. Soon, people even began to expect that a great painter might be just as good at carving sculptures, designing buildings, writing poems – and just about anything else you might think of.

Michelangelo had to design his own highly complex scaffolding system for painting this lofty ceiling, so that the beams wouldn't leave holes in his painting.

Superhuman strengths

Michelangelo Buonarroti, another Florentine artist, was also a man of many talents. His most famous painting covered the ceiling of a vast room in Rome – the Sistine Chapel. It took him four years, perched on towering wooden scaffolding, with the paint dripping into his face and a death-defying drop to the floor. But he was a superb sculptor and an amazing architect, too. When he was only 20 years old, he created a statue in such a perfect imitation of the classical style, it was sold as a genuine antique. Michelangelo also helped to design St. Peter's in Rome, the largest and most important church in Europe.

Michelangelo carved his most impressive sculpture – showing the Biblical hero David – from a block of stone so big that no other sculptor dared to tackle it.

This 17th-century Dutch painting shows a maid quietly pouring milk in a simple room. The full painting is shown on page 48.

High Drama
and
Quiet Lives

In the 16th century, artists became involved in a massive religious split that divided Europe. In northern Europe, some people worried that religious leaders had become corrupt, so they set up their own churches with strict new rules, and banned all religious pictures. Meanwhile, in southern Europe, paintings still filled the churches. Painters everywhere were forced to adapt. In the North, they painted more and more non-religious pictures and scenes of everyday life, while in the South, they made religious paintings bolder and more dramatic than ever.

In parts of Europe, many religious paintings were destroyed.

From
1520

The Reformation

For hundreds of years, painters in Europe had taken it for granted that their most important job was to produce religious pictures. But fierce religious debates forced them to think again. Protesters in northern Europe argued that religious leaders had become too interested in all forms of luxury and display – including paintings. They believed pictures distracted people from praying, instead of helping them, and thought that the money spent on art would be better used helping to feed the poor.

This dramatic painting, made while religious arguments raged across Europe, shows the Bible story of Abraham, who believed he had to sacrifice his son, Isaac. Here, an angel is telling Abraham to release his son.

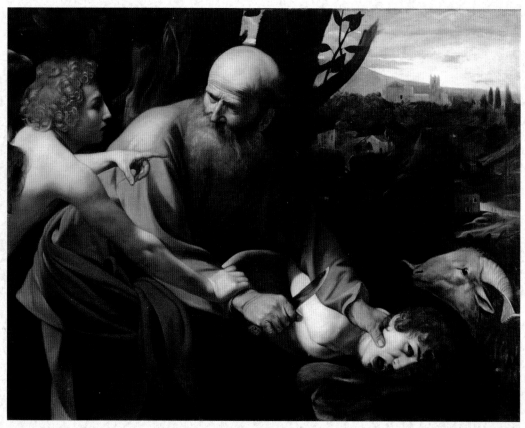

The Sacrifice of Isaac by Michelangelo Merisi (known as Caravaggio). Oil paint on canvas, Italian, 1603.

44

The Pope – the leader of the Catholic Church, which
dominated most of Europe at that time – didn't
agree. So the protestors broke away, and set up new
churches for themselves. The protestors became
known as Protestants, and the entire period became
known as the Reformation.

Bonfire of
religious art

Painting from a
church altar

The great divide

Straight away, the Protestants banned paintings
from their churches, and destroyed all the
religious art they could find, by smashing it or
hiding it under coats of white paint. As religious
pictures became so unpopular in Protestant
countries, artists there had to turn to other subjects.
Classical paintings, portraits and landscapes were
already in fashion. But painters soon started
producing carefully arranged scenes of ordinary
people and household objects, too.

In England in the 1640s,
Protestants destroyed so
much religious art from
the medieval and
Renaissance periods that
there is hardly any left in
English churches today.

Meanwhile, in southern Europe, painters kept
on painting even bigger and more striking religious
pictures – as a snub to the Protestants. They gave
their figures violent gestures and rugged looks, and
added startling contrasts between dark shadows
and bright highlights. Some artists, like Italian
painter Caravaggio, made such forceful religious
paintings that even Catholics began to feel things
had gone too far. Caravaggio gave many of
his Bible characters puzzled, almost ugly
faces – so that some people thought they
no longer looked holy enough. You can
see this in the painting opposite.

Caravaggio, a painter
from Italy, made dramatic
religious pictures, and his
temper was just as wild. He
once flung hot artichokes
at a waiter, and killed a
man in a fight.

Hot-tempered
painter

Hot artichokes

From painters to diplomats

Although some painters like Caravaggio were decidedly shady characters, by the middle of the 16th century painting was becoming a respected profession. Influential patrons treated their favourite artists as friends. Sometimes they even asked painters to carry important messages, or arrange tricky deals, when they visited powerful patrons in other countries.

Dummies in costumes

Painters worked for some patrons who were so important, they didn't have time to sit for days while their portraits were painted. To save time, artists painted the costumes from dummies.

Royal connections

Peter Paul Rubens was a successful painter with a vast workshop in Antwerp (now in Belgium) producing paintings for kings and queens all over Europe. But he also found time for a spot of diplomacy when it was needed. In 1630, he was sent by King Philip IV of Spain to persuade the English king, Charles I, to sign a peace treaty. While he was in England, Rubens made a painting for King Charles called *Peace and War*, showing the advantages of peace. This must have helped, as Charles eventually signed on the dotted line.

Some lucky painters found lifelong jobs with wealthy patrons. Spanish painter Diego Velázquez was the Spanish royal family's official painter from 1622 until his death in 1660, and his main job was painting portraits. King Philip IV had rather unfortunate features – bulging eyes and a massive chin – but luckily, Velázquez was skilled at making his portraits look both lifelike and flattering. In one unusual

Diplomat and painter Rubens coped with some tricky situations. When two paintings he was taking as a royal gift were damaged by rain, he hastily painted a new one.

Speedy brushwork

Soggy paintings

46

portrait (below) Velázquez showed himself painting
at his easel, with members of the royal household
around him. This hints at how close he was to royalty,
but also shows that this was just part of his job.

The Family of Philip IV by Diego Velázquez.
Oil paint on canvas, Spanish, around 1656.

This portrait shows a
young Spanish princess
with her servants. The
king and queen are
reflected in a mirror on
the back wall — perhaps
they have come to watch
their daughter have her
portrait painted.

The first picture dealers

Wealthy patrons often paid good money, but they also had a lot of control over what – and how – their chosen artist painted. Even so, many artists, especially in northern Europe, were beginning to choose their own styles and subjects. This gave them more freedom, but they still had to find someone to buy the finished painting if they wanted to earn a living.

Soon enough, enterprising traders set themselves up as art dealers, finding buyers for paintings – for a fee, of course. But even the most talented artists sometimes had problems selling their pictures.

In this scene, a maid is shown pouring milk from a jug into a bowl. The bread on the table in front of her hints that she is in the middle of preparing a meal.

Scenes showing ordinary people going about their daily lives were becoming popular at the time this picture was created. They are known as "genre" paintings.

Vermeer, who painted this picture, was an expert in peaceful scenes like this. He painted them in a room in his house in the Dutch town of Delft.

The Milkmaid by Jan Vermeer. Oil paint on canvas, Dutch, about 1658-60.

Struggling genius

Rembrandt Harmensz van Rijn found success in his
twenties, as a fashionable portrait-painter in
Amsterdam, in the Netherlands. But then his
portraits fell out of fashion and he turned to other
subjects – from stirring religious scenes to expressive
self-portraits. Rembrandt's son was an art dealer and
sold many of his father's religious paintings, but
Rembrandt's early popularity never returned. Even
so, his pictures, particularly his self-portraits, are
now thought to be some of the finest ever painted.

Surprised expression   Sketch

Self-portraits

As well as creating serious
self-portraits, Dutch artist
Rembrandt also painted
himself pulling faces, to try
out different expressions
and moods.

Scenes of home life

Jan Vermeer was another superb Dutch painter.
Although he was also an art dealer, he had money
worries throughout his career. He only ever finished
about 40 small paintings, which were all quiet scenes
of Dutch life, painted in a very realistic style almost
like photographs.

Experts think Vermeer used a very early type of
camera, called a *camera obscura*, to help him plan his
paintings. He probably set up a
scene in his studio, used a
glass lens to project an
image of the scene onto
his canvas and then
sketched around it.

This picture shows how
a camera obscura may
have worked. Light
passes from a bright
main room through a
lens, into a dark cubicle
and onto a canvas.

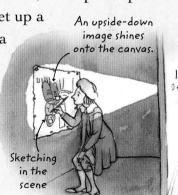

An upside-down
image shines
onto the canvas.

Light
travels
through
a glass
lens here.

Light enters
here.

Sketching
in the
scene

Inside the camera obscura
(Latin for "dark room"), the
artist roughed out the scene,
but painted in the details later.

Crowd-pleasers

To make sure that their paintings would sell well, many painters opted for subjects they knew would be popular – and there were plenty to choose from. Landscape paintings and scenes showing ordinary people and household objects were especially fashionable. These were often painted on fairly small pieces of light, flexible canvas, which made them easy to transport. Now, art lovers could buy pictures from right across Europe, and some artists – and some painting styles – found international fame.

Everyday life

In the past, ordinary people and objects weren't usually considered interesting enough to put into paintings, unless they were part of a particular story. But now, more and more artists were creating scenes showing life in ordinary homes and villages, with people doing everyday things, such as eating, dancing or making music.

Some of the most popular paintings of this period had no people in them at all – they just showed things that people had in their homes, arranged into attractive designs and painted with glowing colours and subtle textures. They were known as "still lifes" and there were many different types – from kitchen scenes showing succulent ingredients to flower paintings with vases of luscious blooms. Still life paintings often had hidden meanings – you can see some examples on the left.

Expensive lobster

Imported lemon

Still life paintings often had hidden meanings. Those showing exotic foods...

Silver cup

Fine glass

...and beautifully crafted tableware hinted that the painting's owner was wealthy.

Music book

Books and music showed the owners of the painting were well-educated...

Candle snuffer

Skull

...and skulls and snuffed candles meant they thought deeply about life and death.

Still Life with Flowers by Rachel Ruysch. Oil paint on canvas, Dutch, before 1750.

This still life painting showing flowers, fruit and insects was made by a Dutch woman painter.

The flowers and fruit shown here could never really be on a table together, because they grow at different times of year.

The painter used this impossible combination of flowers and fruit to remind her viewers how fast things grow, but also how quickly they die.

The tourist trade

By the 17th century, wealthy art lovers began to visit Europe regularly to see famous landmarks and works of art. They tended to follow a well-worn route known as the Grand Tour, and often bought pictures to take home with them, especially landscapes that reminded them of their visit. Claude Gellée, a landscape painter who lived in Italy, sold many of his delicate, airy scenes in this way. Other landscape painters specialized in vivid city scenes, showing bustling streets and famous landmarks.

The landscape style created by Claude was so popular that a type of tinted mirror, or Claude glass, was produced, to make real landscapes look more like Claude's harmonious paintings.

Claude glass   Reflection of landscape

Mr. and Mrs. Andrews by
Thomas Gainsborough. Oil
paint on canvas, British,
about 1748-9.

British painter
Gainsborough, who
painted this portrait of a
fashionable landowner
and his wife, became a
successful member of the
art academy in London.

From
1700

Exhibitions and academies

By the beginning of the 18th century, more people
were buying art than ever before, and painters were
constantly trying to dream up ingenious ways of
advertising their work to these new buyers.

In cities such as London and Paris, artists began
to band together to form art academies, which
organized public art exhibitions. These exhibitions
helped the careers of new, young artists as well as
established ones. One painter who made his name in
this way was Jean-Antoine Watteau, who sent a
painting of an imaginary outdoor scene to the Paris
academy in 1717. It didn't fit any of the categories of
paintings that were usually displayed, but the
academy members loved it and accepted it anyway.
In no time, imaginary landscapes were all the rage.

In and out of fashion

The academy exhibitions were a great success. Fashionable crowds flocked to them, as much to be seen there as to buy paintings. The academies also helped to train young painters, and this was the beginning of art colleges. But, by the end of the 18th century, most academy artists were painting similar subjects – often portraits of the rich and famous – in a similar style. These paintings sold well, but they were not very original, and most artists who did try out new ideas and techniques had their pictures rejected.

Even some successful academy painters began to feel frustrated. Thomas Gainsborough painted more than 700 portraits, but no one would buy the landscape paintings he loved. So, in 1784, he left the London academy in disgust. He was not the only painter who felt it was time for a change.

Broccoli trees

Mirror lake

Gainsborough often tried out different landscape arrangements, using vegetables, mirrors and pebbles, to sketch from.

Academy exhibitions were grand occasions for selling pictures. Some visitors bought the paintings on show; others hired the artists to paint for them.

Wealthy art lovers

Fashionable couple

Fashionable portrait

This British sea painting shows an
old-fashioned sailing ship being towed
away by a new, steam-driven tugboat.
The full painting is shown on page 58.

A revolutionary painter
working out of doors

Revolution

At the end of the 18th century, there were violent revolutions in France and America as people fought to overthrow their rulers and create a new and fairer world. Groundbreaking new inventions were also changing the way people worked and travelled, as factories sprang up in cities and railways raced through the countryside. Many painters felt a new kind of art was needed, to match the harshness and excitement of this new era.

From
1800

Change and rebellion

The late 18th century was a time of wars and violent uprisings. In a bloody revolt in 1789, the French people overthrew their king and the rich and corrupt aristocrats who had ruled their country. In America, too, settlers successfully fought off their British rulers and finally declared their independence.

This mood of rebellion soon spread, although it didn't always lead to violence. All around the world, people began to challenge old ideas and governments, and demand better conditions for ordinary people.

This painting shows French soldiers executing unarmed Spanish civilians. The painter, Goya, wanted everyone to see how bloody and brutal war was.

Execution of the Defenders of Madrid, 3rd May, 1808 by Francisco de Goya. Oil paint on canvas, Spanish, 1818.

Painting the news

Painters had a vital part to play in all this. In those days – before photography was invented – drawing and painting were the only ways of showing people what was going on in the world.

Some artists decided that, instead of painting well-dressed aristocrats, or pretty landscapes, they would create dramatic scenes showing the world-shaking events that were happening around them. To do this, artists had to become like newspaper reporters – keeping an eye on the news for good stories, researching the facts behind them and interviewing eyewitnesses.

Often the resulting paintings showed violent, frightening scenes, because the painters wanted to shock people into thinking hard about what was going on in the world.

Shipwreck survivor

Notes and sketches

Before French painter Théodore Géricault painted a picture of a recent shipwreck, he interviewed survivors to get a clear idea of what had happened.

Lessons from history

Some artists looked to events far back in history, rather than recent news stories, for their inspiration. But they often chose past scenes – such as wars or political struggles – which somehow echoed present problems, and allowed them to express their views on current affairs. Even so, they tried to make their paintings as accurate as possible by researching the correct historical costumes and settings.

Dramatic stories, plays and poems – some ancient, some more recent – and even dreams and fantasies also provided inspiration.

Lurking fears and nightmares

Spanish painter Goya often blended real events with nightmarish visions from his imagination to express his horror at the state of the world.

The 'Fighting Temeraire' tugged to her Last Berth to be broken up, 1838 by Joseph Mallord William Turner. Oil paint on canvas, British, 1839.

This painting shows a famous old sailing ship being towed away for scrap by a new steam-driven tugboat.

Paint

Small palette

Some artists tied up their paints in containers made from pigs' bladders, so they could work outdoors.

Machines and inventions

The 18th century wasn't just a time of political revolutions. Britain was leading a dramatic transformation in technology, which became known as the Industrial Revolution. All kinds of brand-new machines were being invented – from steam trains to mechanical weaving looms – which changed the way people worked, travelled, and even thought.

They also had a massive impact on the landscape. As factories sprang up, transforming towns into cities, and railways spread out through the countryside, landscape painters started painting pictures that celebrated new technology, as well as natural beauty.

Old versus new

British painter Joseph Turner often put the latest steam boats and trains into his paintings, alongside dramatic stormclouds or brilliant sunsets.

In many of his pictures, Turner showed how he felt about changing technology, too. In *The 'Fighting Temeraire'* (opposite), the stately sailing ship is painted in intricate shapes and pale, ghostly colours, while the sturdy steam boat is made from solid blocks of dark, warm paint. This seems to hint that Turner was sad to see beautiful, old things fading away, but excited by the power and energy of the new machines.

Sketching in a storm

Turner was fascinated by wild seascapes. According to one story, he once had himself tied to a ship's mast during a storm, so he could record how it looked.

New perspectives

To reflect the changes around them, painters like Turner also looked for new ways of painting. They were doing more sketching and painting outdoors than ever before, to give their work an authentic feel, and they were also beginning to question old painting tricks, such as aerial perspective (see page 39).

British painter John Constable wanted to paint the landscape as it really looked, and spent hours drawing and painting in the open air – even though this meant carrying his paints around in pigs' bladders, which often leaked. He disagreed with the old idea that everything in the foreground of a landscape painting should be brown. So he once laid a brown violin on some bright green grass, just to prove to a fellow painter how different the colours were.

Bag of brushes   Portable paintbox

Landscape painter Constable liked to sketch outside every day, to study the clouds and sky.

From
1850

Black cloth to
block out light

Early
camera

Early photography
equipment was bulky
and expensive...

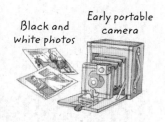

Black and
white photos

Early portable
camera

...but by 1888 smaller,
more affordable cameras
were available...

Colour
photos

Flexible film

...and by 1906, colour
photos and rolls of
film had arrived.

The invention of photography

The invention that had the most dramatic impact on painters was photography. In its early days, taking and developing photographs was very awkward, but, by the 1840s, photographers were able to create pictures quickly and easily. Soon, all sorts of people were buying their own cameras and snapping away. Some artists worried that no one would want paintings any more. But they soon realized they could use paint to capture imaginary scenes and express ideas and feelings in ways that no camera could.

The Pre-Raphaelite Brotherhood

One group of British painters decided they would only paint pictures with a strong message or idea behind them – something they felt paintings had been losing ever since the time of the Renaissance painter Raphael. They called themselves the Pre-Raphaelite Brotherhood, and painted scenes that told stories, often taken from plays or poems set far back in history. They used very bright, clear colours inspired by medieval art, and painted everything in incredible detail, in an ultra-lifelike style.

Symbols and feelings

Meanwhile, other painters were creating mysterious scenes from their imaginations, full of things that had special meanings for them. These artists became known as Symbolists – from the word "symbol",

Cloud shapes

Doodles

meaning a figure, object, colour or anything else that stands for particular feelings and ideas.

In *White Pegasus* by French Symbolist painter Odilon Redon (below), the horse, the mountain and the serpent all symbolize different aspects of people's minds and feelings. Like many Symbolist pictures, and other paintings of the time, this scene is also inspired by ancient myths and legends.

Odilon Redon is supposed to have been inspired by watching clouds and the different shapes they made.

This painting shows a winged horse on top of a mountain, with a serpent at the bottom.

The painter, Redon, was inspired by ancient myths about a magic winged horse called Pegasus and a deadly serpent.

The animals also had their own special meanings for Redon. Pegasus is a symbol for the pure spirit inside each person. The serpent represents people's bad thoughts and feelings.

White Pegasus by Odilon Redon. Oil paint on canvas, French, around 1908.

61

Metal
tube

Oil
paint

Screw-on cap

By the early 1840s, artists
could buy ready-mixed
paint in resealable
metal tubes.

The painting below
shocked many people
when it was first exhibited,
because it looked rough
and sketchy compared to
traditional paintings.

*Impression: Sunrise, Le
Havre* by Claude Monet.
Oil paint on canvas,
French, 1872.

Broader brushstrokes

The invention of photography not only encouraged artists to put more of their feelings and ideas into paint, it also allowed them to stop worrying so much about creating very lifelike pictures. If cameras could capture scenes with perfect accuracy, there was no need for paintings to do this any more.

So some painters began to use bolder brushstrokes, laying the paint onto the canvas in rough patches of colour. Compared to the smooth, even surface of paintings in the past, this looked messy and unfinished to many people. But, seen from just a little way away, the patches blended together into recognizable scenes.

The Impressionists

The new style of painting did not go down well at the official exhibitions. French painter Edouard Manet was accused of painting in smears, and his work was rejected by the main Paris art show, along with paintings by many of his friends.

In 1874, some of Manet's young friends became so frustrated, they set up their own exhibition instead. One painting stood out from all the others – *Impression: Sunrise, Le Havre*. The painter, Claude Monet, wanted to capture an impression of the colours and shapes in the misty seaport of Le Havre. Soon, Monet and many of his friends were being called Impressionists, after Monet's picture.

Removing leaves

Painting outdoors

French artist Monet liked to paint directly from nature. He once arranged for some trees' spring leaves to be removed, so he could finish painting a winter scene.

Colour contrasts

Many Impressionist painters liked to work on entire paintings in the open air, so they could record the changing light and colours of the landscape. Handy, resealable metal paint tubes were now available, which made outdoor painting much easier.

The Impressionists were also interested in scientific theories about colour. They often placed little strokes and dabs of strongly contrasting colours next to one another on the canvas, to make their paintings look more vibrant. Impressionist paintings eventually became very popular, although at first, many people thought they looked crude and clumsy. But, right from the start, the new style excited a whole generation of young painters.

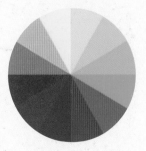

On this colour wheel, colours that contrast most strongly are shown opposite each other. The Impressionist painters used these contrasting pairs of colours together.

French painter Seurat came up with a way of painting in dots of colour. He was so pleased, he went back and added dots to some of his earlier works.

Dots and dabs

The Impressionists' rapid, dabbing brushstrokes and bright colours inspired many young painters to use similar techniques, although their results were often quite different.

French painter Georges Seurat was fascinated by colour theories, and painted scenes of Parisian life using thousands and thousands of tiny dots of bright, contrasting colours. He realized that, from a little way away, the dots would blur together to look like solid shapes and smoothly blended colours. His technique became known as Pointillism. Like the Impressionists, he used contrasting colours next to each other, but he was more interested in the way the colours looked together than in capturing outdoor light effects.

Putting feelings into paint

Dutch painter van Gogh used paint to express his feelings. When he became depressed and cut off part of his ear, he even painted a self-portrait showing the bandage.

A young Dutch painter called Vincent van Gogh used dashes and swirls of thick paint in bright colours, to put the way he felt about things onto canvas. His striking paintings show many emotions, from happy landscapes, and calm paintings of his bedroom, to restless night scenes. Most people thought his pictures looked childlike and simple, but this was just what he was aiming for. He wanted to find a way of painting about his own feelings, not complicated ideas. But he only ever managed to sell one of his paintings, and became seriously depressed. In 1889, he cut off part of his own ear, and the following year he killed himself.

The simple life

One of van Gogh's close friends, French painter Paul Gauguin, also wanted to find a new, simpler way of painting. His solution was to leave Europe in search of a less complicated way of life – he went to live on the tropical island of Tahiti, where he painted pictures of the local people and scenery. Both Gauguin and van Gogh struggled to sell their paintings, and were often so poor they couldn't even afford paints. But their ideas were ahead of their time, and they had a massive influence on the art of the next century.

Van Gogh's Bedroom at Arles by Vincent van Gogh. Oil paint on canvas, Dutch, 1889.

Van Gogh wanted this painting of his bedroom to feel restful. So he combined soothing blues and greens with cosy reds and yellows, painted in simple strokes.

This is a detail from a painting made during
the First World War. It's an abstract picture
— it doesn't show a recognizable scene.
The full painting is shown on page 71.

Modern Times

The events of the 20th century changed the world forever. The bloodshed of two world wars forced people to rethink everything that was important to them. Meanwhile, new entertainments – photography, radio and television – had arrived for good. Painting also had to change to keep up with the times, and it's still changing today.

An interesting
20th-century way of
making a painting

From
1900

Modern art begins

Over the last 100 years or so, there have been more changes in art than at any other time in history. Different artists have tried out a huge variety of approaches and techniques, in the search for new and original styles.

But painters have also been fascinated by ideas as old as painting itself – such as how to make objects in flat pictures appear more solid, or how to show ideas and feelings in paint.

Mont Sainte-Victoire by Paul Cézanne. Oil paint on canvas, French, 1902-4.

French artist Cézanne painted this mountain over and over again. He tried to show how far away it was, and how solid it looked.

The painting is built up from small patches of colour, which seem to mark out different angles of the mountain, land, trees and houses.

68

Different viewpoints

French painter Paul Cézanne wanted to give his paintings a feeling of space, and make the things in them seem solid. But instead of turning to techniques such as perspective, he studied how human eyes work.

We see things from many different angles, partly because we move around, and partly because we have two eyes, each with a slightly different viewpoint. Cézanne showed this by painting things from many, slightly different angles. The results may look a little disjointed, but this was deliberate. It was meant to reflect the flickering way people really see things, and give a convincing feeling of space.

Cubism

Some artists went even further, painting things as if they were in fragments, each seen from a different position. These paintings seemed to be made up of pyramids, cones and cubes, so the style became known as Cubism.

Spanish artist Pablo Picasso made many Cubist paintings, but he was also inspired by traditional African masks and carvings. He felt they had a power that European art had lost. Picasso combined their simple shapes and bold colours with Cubist ideas, and produced some of the most original paintings ever made.

One picture by Spanish artist Picasso, inspired by African masks, looked so startling and new that it wasn't exhibited for 30 years. Now it's seen as a masterpiece. It's called The Ladies of Avignon.

African masks

Sketches

Dancing figure

Block of colour

Bright colours, flat shapes

Some painters went in the opposite direction to Cubism. They decided that, as paintings really are flat, they might as well paint in a way that emphasized this. Their pictures are full of simple shapes and bright colours, and often look more like flat patterns than lifelike scenes.

Going abstract

Henri Matisse, a French painter, was fascinated by colours and patterns. Often, he painted scenes that included decorative fabrics and wallpapers, to underline the fact that the other things he painted were like patterns, too. Later in life, Matisse began to make pictures by cutting shapes from coloured paper. Some of these hardly had any recognizable subject at all – he mainly enjoyed the colours and shapes.

Even before Matisse was making his cutouts, other painters had started arranging colours and shapes to be enjoyed just for their own sake. A Russian artist named Vassily Kandinsky was probably the first to do this, but others soon followed, including Kasimir Malevich, another Russian painter.

French painter Matisse made many pictures of dancers, including a massive painting 14m (47ft) long, made up of flat blocks of colour.

Paper

Glue

Many 20th-century artists created pictures called "collages" by glueing down paper or cardboard...

String

Bottle tops

...or more unusual materials.

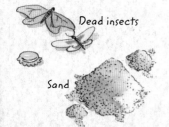

Dead insects

Sand

This type of painting, which didn't represent anything beyond colours and shapes, became known as "abstract" art. Many abstract painters believed their art could reach people's ideas and feelings directly, as music does.

Fallen painting

When Kandinsky saw a painting the wrong way up, he still enjoyed its shapes and colours. This inspired him to make the first abstract paintings.

This abstract painting uses shapes and colours to create a design that isn't meant to look like any recognizable scene.

The painter, Malevich, wanted to create art that was beyond everything natural and ordinary. He called his art "Suprematist", because it was about ideas he thought were "supremely" important.

Suprematist Composition by Kasimir Malevich. Oil paint on canvas, Russian, 1915.

This picture from the First World War shows wounded soldiers being carried on horse-drawn stretchers known as travoys.

The British government asked the artist, Spencer, to paint a record of what he had seen and felt during the war.

War painting

The first half of the 20th century brought the two most disastrous and bloody wars in history: the First World War, from 1914-18, and the Second World War, from 1939-45. By the time the fighting ended, millions of soldiers and ordinary men, women and children had lost their lives. Many artists were among the dead. Those who survived knew that life would never be the same again, and many of them created brave, sometimes shocking images, to help them face up to the terrible things that had happened.

Travoys arriving with wounded at a dressing station, Smol, Macedonia, 1916 by Stanley Spencer. Oil paint on canvas, British, 1919.

Dali
suffocating

Strange art

But some artists felt there was no normal way to respond to the terrible fighting or the chaos that followed it, and set about making art that seemed strange and disturbing. During the First World War, a group of artists who called themselves "Dada" began sticking together fragments of everyday objects to make pictures and sculptures that looked deliberately messy and meaningless.

This inspired another group, known as the Surrealists. They painted lifelike pictures of ordinary objects in impossible situations – but their scenes do look real in an odd, dream-like way. "Surreal" means "more than real". The Surrealists felt that, like dreams or fantasies, their paintings could add something extra to everyday reality, and express powerful feelings that were usually ignored.

Surrealist artists did some bizarre things. Spanish Surrealist Salvador Dalí once gave a speech dressed in a diving suit – but he started suffocating and had to be rescued.

Burning paintings

Both these types of art provoked a strong reaction. The Nazis, who rose to power in Germany in the 1930s, persecuted everyone who didn't support their brutal ideas – and this included artists who disliked war, or who rejected the traditional, realistic style of painting. Right up to their fall from power in 1945, the Nazis banned certain artists from selling their work or teaching art, and even burned their paintings.

It took years for Europe to recover fully from the two world wars. Meanwhile, on the other side of the world, exciting things were starting to happen...

Many artists left Europe to get away from the effects of the Second World War, and headed for a new life in the USA.

Statue of Liberty

Excited European artist

73

From
1950

US artist Jackson Pollock covered huge canvases with rhythmical splatters of household paint — sometimes poured straight from the tin.

Household paint

Big paintbrush

The new abstract art

For many people in the years after the Second World War, life was getting better. New factories poured out masses of cars, refrigerators and other useful goods, while radio, cinema and television provided exciting entertainment. Artists felt a new age had begun, and looked for new ways of painting to celebrate it.

Abstract paintings, made up of bold shapes and colours, seemed to catch the mood. This was especially true in the American city of New York, which was full of painters, many of whom had left Europe because of the war. Some painters decided to concentrate on how to express feelings through abstract paintings – so their art became known as

Sheng-Tung by Bridget Riley. Acrylic paint on linen, British, 1974.

This abstract painting is designed to work like an optical illusion.

The curving lines make the canvas look as if it is wavy, not flat, and the subtle colour contrasts seem to shimmer with movement.

This type of painting became known as Op art, from the word "optical".

Abstract Expressionism. One American Abstract Expressionist, Jackson Pollock, put his paint on in energetic splashes and drips, while another, Mark Rothko, painted huge coloured shapes designed to have a calm, uplifting feel.

Optical illusions

Before long, artists elsewhere were taking abstract painting in even more directions. For example, British painter Bridget Riley was inspired by the colour theories of the Impressionists and their followers. She used stripes and spots in contrasting shades to paint pictures that seem to pulse with movement – and she's still creating similar paintings today.

Body print

French painter Yves Klein asked models to cover themselves in paint and roll on paper. The pictures looked interesting, but Klein felt that making them was a work of art in itself.

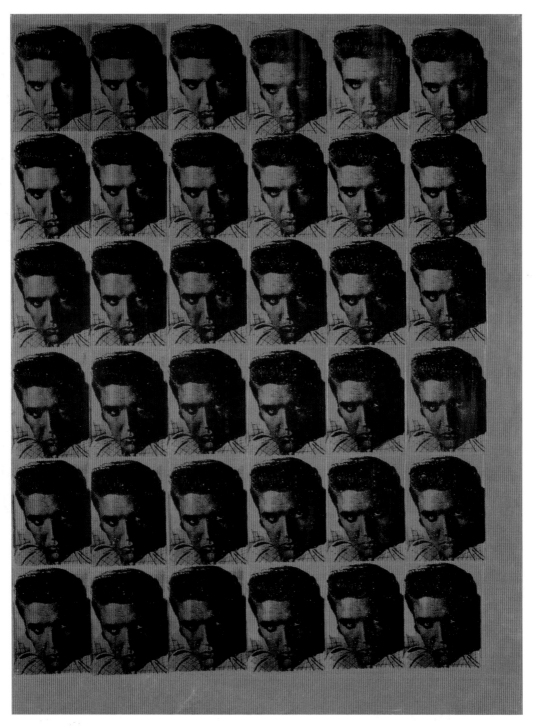

Red Elvis by Andy Warhol. Screenprint, American, 1962.

This print was made using ink and a photograph of singer Elvis Presley. Elvis looks slightly different in each copy of the photograph, showing that mass-produced images can be unique, too.

Modern technology

In the 1960s and 70s, advances in technology made painters think again about what painting was there for. New printing methods meant that colour copies of great paintings could be reproduced in their thousands in books and as posters. Suddenly, paintings no longer seemed unique. This was a big shock for some painters, but others began to play with the idea of machine-made pictures. They drew their inspiration from popular, or "pop", culture, so their art became known as Pop art.

British Pop artist Peter Blake designed an album cover for the famous pop group, The Beatles. Blake arranged life-size cutouts of famous people among plants and other props, and then photographed them.

Mass media

US Pop artist Andy Warhol created pictures using advertising images and photographs, which he printed or stencilled so he could repeat the images as often as he liked. He called his studio The Factory, because he mass-produced his pictures. But, in fact, everything was printed by hand, so there were subtle differences between each copy. Each of Warhol's works was unique, just like traditional paintings.

Another American Pop artist, Roy Lichtenstein, painted huge cartoony pictures that looked like printed comics. He even painted in thousands of tiny dots, to look like the marks made by colour printing. This was a jokey way of getting people to think about the differences between mass-produced images and paintings. Lichtenstein and other painters also used a brand new kind of paint, called acrylic. Made from plastic, it dries fast and gives very even colours.

Bottle of acrylic paint

Plastic-based acrylic paints first went on sale in the 1950s, but it was in the 1960s that they really caught on.

Acrylic paint in tubes

Painting now

In recent years, painting has been as popular as ever, but many artists have also been experimenting with new ways of making pictures. Photocopiers, scanners and computers have all been used to help make paintings, or to make images that are displayed alongside paintings as works of art in their own right.

More new technology

Some people might think it's cheating to use cameras and computers to help make paintings and drawings, but really, making use of new technology is nothing new for painters. Ever since prehistoric times, they've been using the most up-to-date tools they could find. And a camera or a computer can be used just as creatively as paint and a paintbrush.

Now, in the 21st century, there are plenty of artists doing what painters have always done – making pictures about the world around them, their feelings and ideas.

Who knows what artists will think of next...

Empire State Building

Movie camera

US artist Andy Warhol tried all sorts of mechanical ways of creating images. He even made a movie of the Empire State Building that went on for eight hours.

Finished picture

Print out

British artist David Hockney is famous for his paintings, but also makes collages from photos, and uses fax machines to make some of his pictures.

Fax machine

Factfile

Read on, to find out more about looking at paintings and discovering further information on the Internet. You'll also find a painting timeline and a glossary to explain any difficult or unusual words.

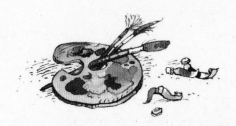

Looking at paintings

There are lots of different places to find paintings.
You can look at photographs of them in books like
this one, or on the Internet, and you can visit them
in museums and art galleries all around the world.
You might even have a real painting hanging in
your home – even if it's not a famous one.

Looking at a real painting is an exciting experience. The colours seem
fresher and brighter, and you can see all the textures of the paint.

Finding clues

Paintings come in all sorts of different shapes, sizes and styles.
You could look out for clues, to help you find out more about
each picture, and discover how it fits into the story of
painting. Labels next to pictures usually tell you the basics,
such as the name of the artist, the date the painting was made
and the type of paints that were used. Most galleries, books
and websites display this information near each painting.

Internet links

There are lots of websites with activities to help you find out more about different painters and their paintings. At the Usborne Quicklinks Website you'll find links to some great sites where you can:

- ✹ visit art galleries and museums around the world

- ✹ make a portrait of your family or best friend

- ✹ become an art detective and solve a mystery

- ✹ try out lots of painting and drawing projects for yourself

- ✹ learn more about paints and pigments

- ✹ visit Leonardo da Vinci's workshop

- ✹ find out how an oil painting is made

Discover lots of projects for making your own drawings and paintings, with helpful step-by-step instructions.

For links to these sites, go to the Usborne Quicklinks Website at **www.usborne-quicklinks.com** and enter the keywords "story of painting".

When using the Internet, please follow the Internet safety guidelines shown on the Usborne Quicklinks Website. The links at Usborne Quicklinks are regularly reviewed and updated, but Usborne Publishing is not responsible and does not accept liability for the content on any website other than its own. We recommend that children are supervised while using the Internet.

Find out about the world's great museums and galleries, and plan a real – or virtual – visit.

Timeline

This timeline lists the main landmarks in the story of painting, alongside some important dates in history. You can also see where all the paintings shown in this book fit in.

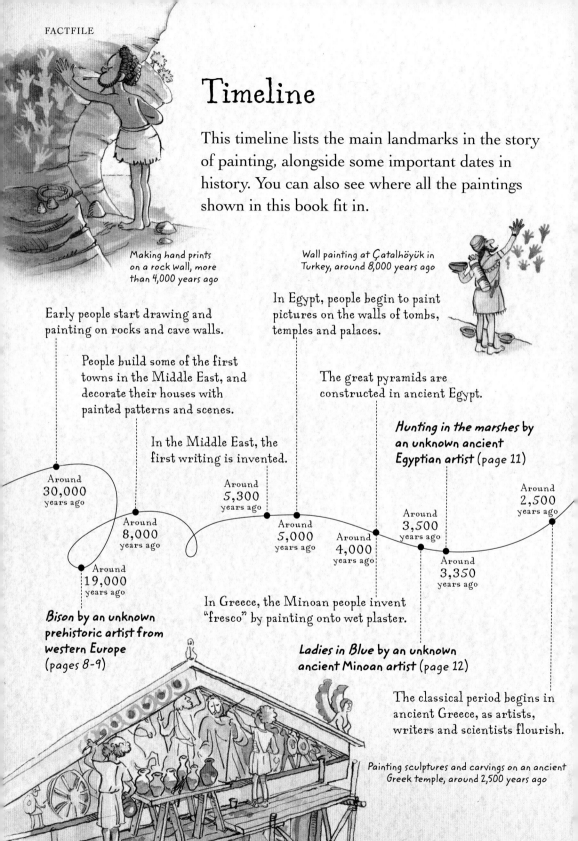

Making hand prints on a rock wall, more than 4,000 years ago

Wall painting at Çatalhöyük in Turkey, around 8,000 years ago

Early people start drawing and painting on rocks and cave walls.

In Egypt, people begin to paint pictures on the walls of tombs, temples and palaces.

People build some of the first towns in the Middle East, and decorate their houses with painted patterns and scenes.

The great pyramids are constructed in ancient Egypt.

In the Middle East, the first writing is invented.

Hunting in the marshes by an unknown ancient Egyptian artist (page 11)

Around 30,000 years ago

Around 8,000 years ago

Around 5,300 years ago

Around 5,000 years ago

Around 4,000 years ago

Around 3,500 years ago

Around 3,350 years ago

Around 2,500 years ago

Around 19,000 years ago

Bison by an unknown prehistoric artist from western Europe (pages 8-9)

In Greece, the Minoan people invent "fresco" by painting onto wet plaster.

Ladies in Blue by an unknown ancient Minoan artist (page 12)

The classical period begins in ancient Greece, as artists, writers and scientists flourish.

Painting sculptures and carvings on an ancient Greek temple, around 2,500 years ago

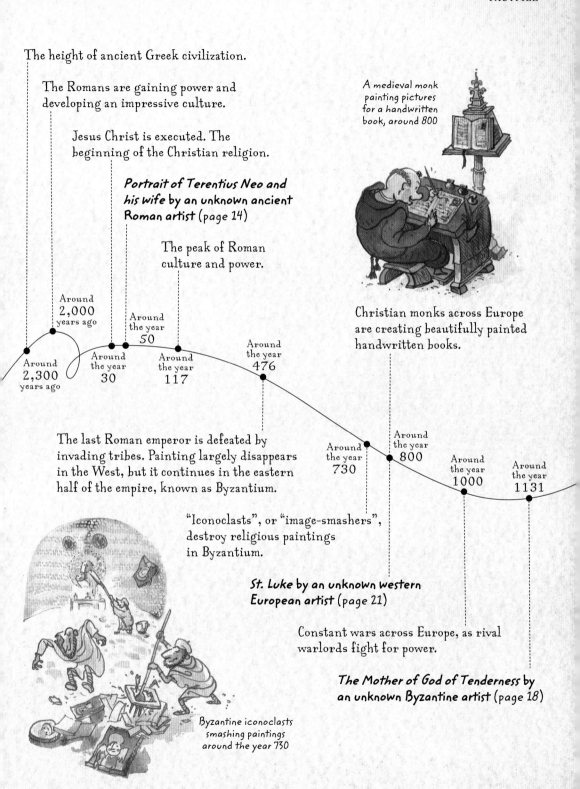

The height of ancient Greek civilization.

The Romans are gaining power and developing an impressive culture.

Jesus Christ is executed. The beginning of the Christian religion.

Portrait of Terentius Neo and his wife by an unknown ancient Roman artist (page 14)

The peak of Roman culture and power.

A medieval monk painting pictures for a handwritten book, around 800

Around 2,300 years ago

Around 2,000 years ago

Around the year 30

Around the year 50

Around the year 117

Around the year 476

Christian monks across Europe are creating beautifully painted handwritten books.

The last Roman emperor is defeated by invading tribes. Painting largely disappears in the West, but it continues in the eastern half of the empire, known as Byzantium.

"Iconoclasts", or "image-smashers", destroy religious paintings in Byzantium.

Around the year 730

Around the year 800

Around the year 1000

Around the year 1131

St. Luke by an unknown western European artist (page 21)

Constant wars across Europe, as rival warlords fight for power.

The Mother of God of Tenderness by an unknown Byzantine artist (page 18)

Byzantine iconoclasts smashing paintings around the year 730

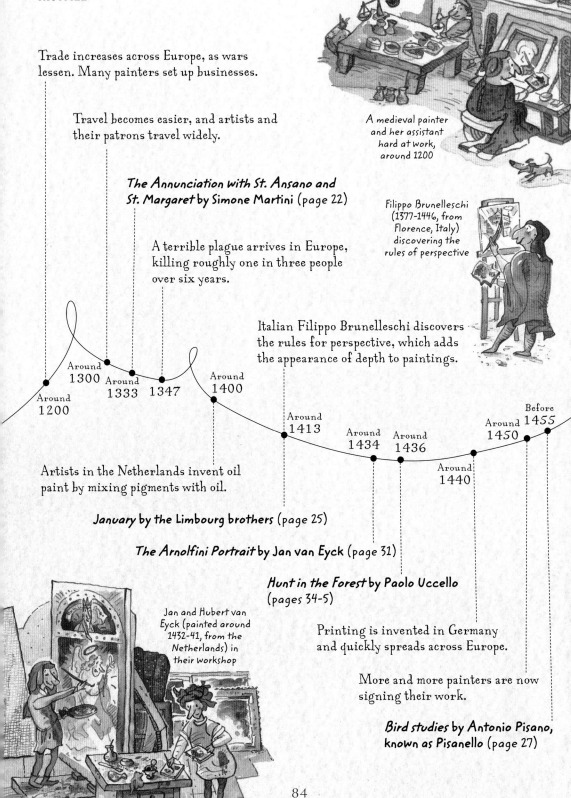

Trade increases across Europe, as wars lessen. Many painters set up businesses.

Travel becomes easier, and artists and their patrons travel widely.

A medieval painter and her assistant hard at work, around 1200

The Annunciation with St. Ansano and St. Margaret by Simone Martini (page 22)

Filippo Brunelleschi (1377-1446, from Florence, Italy) discovering the rules of perspective

A terrible plague arrives in Europe, killing roughly one in three people over six years.

Italian Filippo Brunelleschi discovers the rules for perspective, which adds the appearance of depth to paintings.

Around 1300

Around 1333 1347

Around 1400

Around 1200

Around 1413

Around 1434

Around 1436

Around 1450

Before 1455

Around 1440

Artists in the Netherlands invent oil paint by mixing pigments with oil.

January by the Limbourg brothers (page 25)

The Arnolfini Portrait by Jan van Eyck (page 31)

Hunt in the Forest by Paolo Uccello (pages 34-5)

Jan and Hubert van Eyck (painted around 1432-41, from the Netherlands) in their workshop

Printing is invented in Germany and quickly spreads across Europe.

More and more painters are now signing their work.

Bird studies by Antonio Pisano, known as Pisanello (page 27)

84

In Italy, there is a surge of interest in all things ancient Greek and Roman.

Sandro Botticelli (1444/5-1510, from Florence, Italy) sketching a classical statue

The Birth of Venus by Sandro Botticelli (page 32)

Artists start to study both living people and dead bodies, to make their paintings of figures more accurate.

Around 1470

Italian explorer Christopher Columbus is the first European to reach the West Indies, off the coast of North America.

Around 1485

Around 1490

Artists in Venice, Italy, start to paint on canvas – strong fabric – stretched on wooden frames.

Around 1492

Leonardo da Vinci (1452-1519, from Vinci, near Florence, Italy) testing one of his inventions

Head of a Cherub by Raffaello Sanzio, known as Raphael (page 37)

Around 1500

Around 1503-6

Around 1504-5

Around 1520

Around 1550

Mona Lisa by Leonardo da Vinci (page 40)

The Holy Family by Michelangelo Buonarroti (page 38)

Michelangelo Buonarroti (1475-1564, from Florence, Italy) painting the Sistine Chapel ceiling

In northern Europe, protestors break away from the Catholic Church. They set up their own Protestant churches and ban religious paintings.

A very early type of camera, known as the *camera obscura*, is developed. Artists use it to help rough out their paintings.

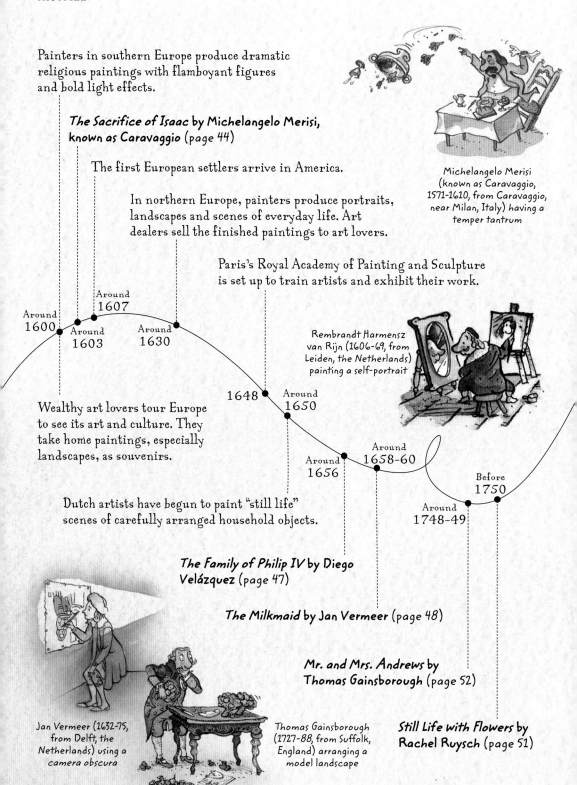

Painters in southern Europe produce dramatic
religious paintings with flamboyant figures
and bold light effects.

The Sacrifice of Isaac by Michelangelo Merisi,
known as Caravaggio (page 44)

The first European settlers arrive in America.

In northern Europe, painters produce portraits,
landscapes and scenes of everyday life. Art
dealers sell the finished paintings to art lovers.

Paris's Royal Academy of Painting and Sculpture
is set up to train artists and exhibit their work.

Michelangelo Merisi
(known as Caravaggio,
1571-1610, from Caravaggio,
near Milan, Italy) having a
temper tantrum

Around
1600

Around
1607

Around
1603

Around
1630

1648

Around
1650

Around
1656

Around
1658-60

Around
1748-49

Before
1750

Rembrandt Harmensz
van Rijn (1606-69, from
Leiden, the Netherlands)
painting a self-portrait

Wealthy art lovers tour Europe
to see its art and culture. They
take home paintings, especially
landscapes, as souvenirs.

Dutch artists have begun to paint "still life"
scenes of carefully arranged household objects.

The Family of Philip IV by Diego
Velázquez (page 47)

The Milkmaid by Jan Vermeer (page 48)

Mr. and Mrs. Andrews by
Thomas Gainsborough (page 52)

Jan Vermeer (1632-75,
from Delft, the
Netherlands) using a
camera obscura

Thomas Gainsborough
(1727-88, from Suffolk,
England) arranging a
model landscape

Still Life with Flowers by
Rachel Ruysch (page 51)

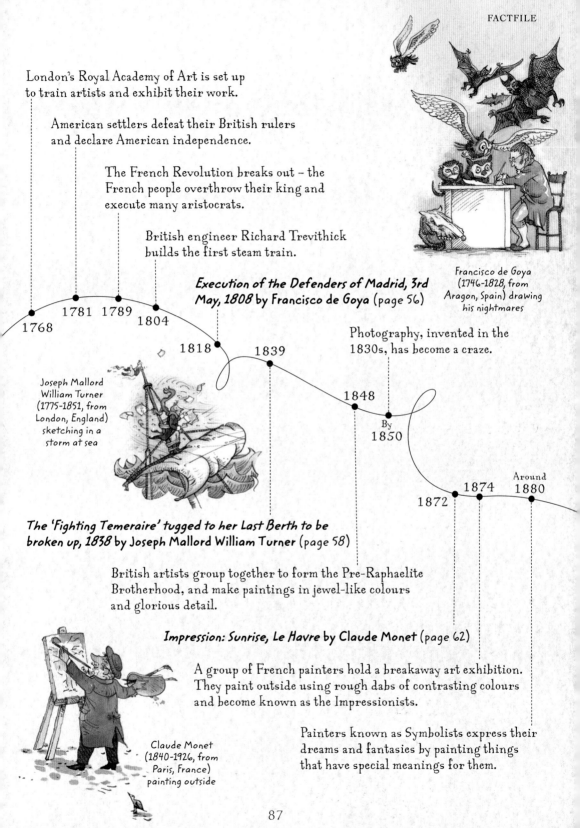

London's Royal Academy of Art is set up to train artists and exhibit their work.

American settlers defeat their British rulers and declare American independence.

The French Revolution breaks out – the French people overthrow their king and execute many aristocrats.

British engineer Richard Trevithick builds the first steam train.

Execution of the Defenders of Madrid, 3rd May, 1808 by Francisco de Goya (page 56)

Francisco de Goya (1746-1828, from Aragon, Spain) drawing his nightmares

Photography, invented in the 1830s, has become a craze.

1768   1781   1789   1804   1818   1839   1848   By 1850   1872   1874   Around 1880

Joseph Mallord William Turner (1775-1851, from London, England) sketching in a storm at sea

The 'Fighting Temeraire' tugged to her Last Berth to be broken up, 1838 by Joseph Mallord William Turner (page 58)

British artists group together to form the Pre-Raphaelite Brotherhood, and make paintings in jewel-like colours and glorious detail.

Impression: Sunrise, Le Havre by Claude Monet (page 62)

A group of French painters hold a breakaway art exhibition. They paint outside using rough dabs of contrasting colours and become known as the Impressionists.

Painters known as Symbolists express their dreams and fantasies by painting things that have special meanings for them.

Claude Monet (1840-1926, from Paris, France) painting outside

87

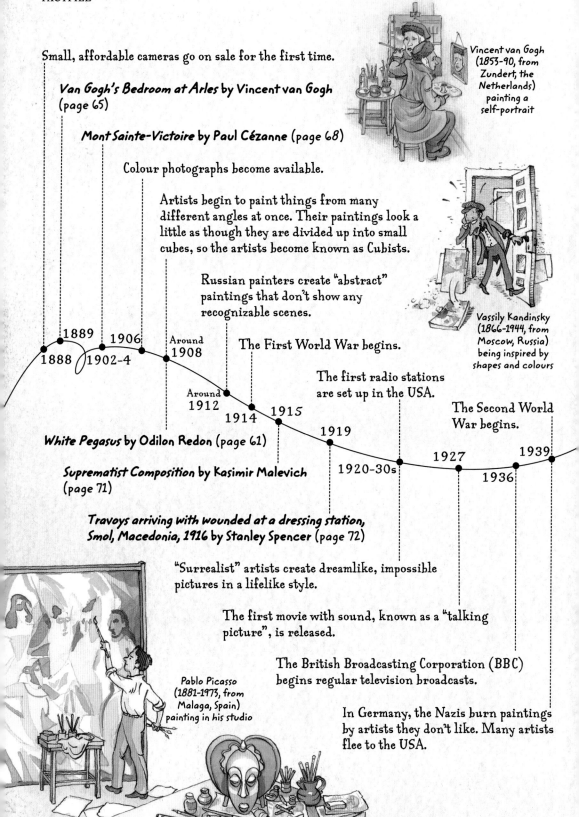

Small, affordable cameras go on sale for the first time.

Van Gogh's Bedroom at Arles by Vincent van Gogh (page 65)

Mont Sainte-Victoire by Paul Cézanne (page 68)

Vincent van Gogh (1853–90, from Zundert, the Netherlands) painting a self-portrait

Colour photographs become available.

Artists begin to paint things from many different angles at once. Their paintings look a little as though they are divided up into small cubes, so the artists become known as Cubists.

Russian painters create "abstract" paintings that don't show any recognizable scenes.

1889   1906   Around
1888 1902-4   1908

The First World War begins.

Vassily Kandinsky (1866–1944, from Moscow, Russia) being inspired by shapes and colours

The first radio stations are set up in the USA.

Around 1912
1914   1915   1919

The Second World War begins.

1927   1939
1920-30s   1936

White Pegasus by Odilon Redon (page 61)

Suprematist Composition by Kasimir Malevich (page 71)

Travoys arriving with wounded at a dressing station, Smol, Macedonia, 1916 by Stanley Spencer (page 72)

"Surrealist" artists create dreamlike, impossible pictures in a lifelike style.

The first movie with sound, known as a "talking picture", is released.

The British Broadcasting Corporation (BBC) begins regular television broadcasts.

Pablo Picasso (1881–1973, from Malaga, Spain) painting in his studio

In Germany, the Nazis burn paintings by artists they don't like. Many artists flee to the USA.

In the USA, painters create striking abstract pictures that express their feelings. These painters become known as Abstract Expressionists.

A new plastic-based type of paint, called acrylic, goes on sale.

Young artists borrow ideas from advertising and popular music to create "Pop" art.

Red Elvis by Andy Warhol (page 76)

US astronauts Neil Armstrong and Buzz Aldrin land on the moon.

More and more artists are using photographs, printing and moving images alongside paintings, or to help make paintings.

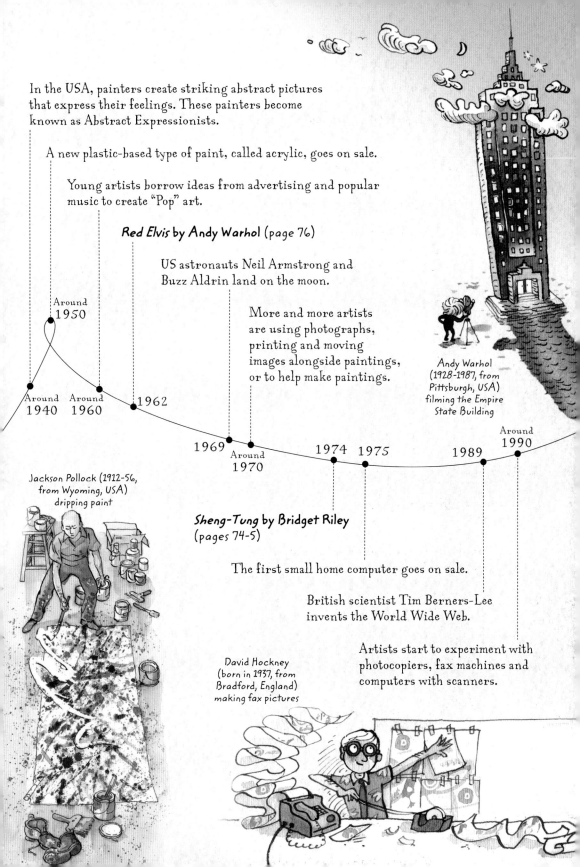

Andy Warhol (1928-1987, from Pittsburgh, USA) filming the Empire State Building

Around 1950

Around 1940

Around 1960

1962

1969

Around 1970

1974

1975

1989

Around 1990

Jackson Pollock (1912-56, from Wyoming, USA) dripping paint

Sheng-Tung by Bridget Riley (pages 74-5)

The first small home computer goes on sale.

British scientist Tim Berners-Lee invents the World Wide Web.

David Hockney (born in 1937, from Bradford, England) making fax pictures

Artists start to experiment with photocopiers, fax machines and computers with scanners.

Glossary

Use this glossary to look up any unfamiliar words you may have come across in the story of painting. Words shown in *italics* also have their own, separate entries.

abstract - art that doesn't show any recognizable people, things or *scenes*.

Abstract Expressionism - a type of *abstract* art designed to express the artist's feelings. It was developed in the USA after the Second World War by artists including Mark Rothko and Jackson Pollock.

academy - see *art academy*

acrylic paint - quick-drying paint made by mixing *pigments* with liquid plastic.

aerial perspective - an illusion of distance created in *landscape paintings* by using pale, blueish colours for distant things and strong, brownish colours for nearby things. Leonardo da Vinci developed the technique.

afterlife - a place where some people believe the dead go to live.

angel - a messenger from God.

Annunciation - a Bible *scene* in which an *angel* tells Jesus's mother, Mary, that she will have a son.

architect - someone who designs buildings.

art academy - an organization set up to promote art.

art dealer - someone who finds buyers for works of art.

baroque - the name given to the bold, dramatic art of 17th-century artists including Caravaggio and Peter Paul Rubens.

Byzantium - the eastern half of the *Roman* empire which included the area that is now Greece, Turkey and the Middle East; anything to do with Byzantium is known as **Byzantine.**

camera obscura - meaning "dark room", it is a simple device for projecting images through a glass lens onto a flat surface.

candle snuffer - a tool designed for putting out candles.

canvas - a type of strong cloth used as a surface for painting.

Catholic - the part of the *Christian* Church run from *Rome* by the *Pope*. People or countries that follow this faith are also known as Catholic.

cave painting - ancient painting found on cave walls or other rock surfaces.

chapel - a small church.

Christian - someone who follows the teachings of Jesus Christ; the religion is known as **Christianity.**

civilization - a sophisticated human society made up of complex cultural, political and legal organizations.

classical - the name for anything from the period when the ancient Greek and *Roman civilizations* were flourishing – starting in Greece around 2,500 years ago.

Claude glass - a tinted mirror designed to make reflected landscapes look like paintings by 17th-century artist Claude Gellée.

Constantinople - the capital city of *Byzantium*; now Istanbul in Turkey.

Cubism - a style of painting, looking like little cubes, developed by artists including Pablo Picasso at the start of the 20th century. The Cubists painted objects as if they were broken up into fragments – each viewed from a different angle – to reflect the way people see things from many different viewpoints.

culture - the ideas, skills and artistic achievements of a people.

Dada - a type of art developed during the First World War by artists including Tristan Tsara and Hugo Ball, who were horrified at the brutality of the fighting. They felt there was no sensible reaction to the war, so they made works that seemed meaningless and strange. "Dada" is French for "rocking-horse"; Dada artists are supposed to have chosen the name at random from a dictionary.

detail - a small part of a painting; anything intricately made is described as **detailed**.

diplomat - someone whose job it is to negotiate for different people and countries; the job is called **diplomacy**.

Dutch - the word used to describe pre-1830 art and artists from the northern, *Protestant* part of the *Netherlands* (including the province of Holland), and all art and artists from the Netherlands after 1830.

egg tempera - quick-drying paint made by mixing *pigments* with egg.

encaustic - waterproof paint made by mixing *pigments* with wax.

exhibition - a show of art works.

Flemish - a word sometimes used to describe pre-1830 art and artists from the southern, *Catholic* part of the *Netherlands*.

Florence - an Italian city; people or things from Florence are known as **Florentine.**

fresco - a type of wall painting made by painting onto wet *plaster.*

genre painting - a type of painting showing *scenes* of everyday life.

gold leaf - real gold beaten into extremely thin sheets.

halo - a bright glow, often painted around the head of an *angel* or *saint* in *medieval* pictures.

icon - meaning "image" in Greek, it's a type of religious painting.

iconoclast - someone who smashes *icons* — like the *Byzantines* who destroyed religious images around 730.

illumination - a brightly painted picture in a *medieval* handwritten book, or *manuscript*; a book containing these paintings is called an **illuminated manuscript**.

Impressionist - a style of art developed in the late 19th century by artists including Claude Monet, using rapid dabs and streaks of bright, contrasting colours. The Impressionists liked to paint entire pictures outside, to capture the changing effects of natural light.

Industrial Revolution - the time in 18th- and 19th-century Britain when many new machines and industrial processes were being invented. This changed the way people worked, travelled and even thought, as new factories sprang up, railways and canals criss-crossed the countryside and more and more people flocked to the growing towns to seek work.

landscape painting - a type of painting showing natural countryside *scenes*.

lapis lazuli - a semi-*precious stone* used to make very expensive blue paint known as ultramarine.

lifelike - looking very similar to real life.

linseed oil - oil from the seed of the flax plant, often used to make *oil paint*.

manuscript - a handwritten book.

martyr - someone who suffers or dies as a witness for their beliefs.

master painter - a painter in charge of a *workshop* and assistants.

medieval - anything to do with the *Middle Ages*, the period of history between the fall of the *Roman* empire (in the 5th century) and the *Renaissance* (around the 15th century).

merchant - someone who makes a living from buying and selling things.

metalpoint - an early type of pencil, made from a sharpened point of lead, silver or other metal, and used for drawing on paper.

Middle Ages - the period of history between the fall of the *Roman* empire (in the 5th century) and the *Renaissance* (around the 15th century).

Minoans - an ancient people who lived in Crete and other parts of Greece, including the Cyclades islands, around 3,500 years ago.

monastery - a place where religious people, such as monks, lead a life of prayer and study together, away from other people.

mud brick - brick made from dried mud.

Netherlands - a country in northern Europe between Germany and France. Before 1830, the Netherlands included Belgium; the world **Netherlandish** is sometimes used to describe art and artists from the entire area before this split. During the *Reformation*, the southern part of the area remained *Catholic*, while the northern part, including the province of Holland, became *Protestant*. See also *Dutch* and *Flemish*.

nude - a painting or statue of a naked figure.

oil paint - slow-drying paint made by mixing *pigments* with oil. Oil paint can be used thickly or in thin, see-through layers.

Op art - a type of abstract art based on *optical illusions*, developed in the 1950s and 60s by artists including Bridget Riley. Op art paintings often use strongly contrasting colours and geometric patterns and shapes.

optical illusion - a drawing or painting that looks like something it isn't, or plays tricks on the eye.

palette - a board used for mixing paints; also the range of colours used in a painting. A **palette knife** is used to spread and mix paints on the palette.

patron - someone who buys art and supports artists.

perspective - a way of marking out space to create a convincing illusion of depth in drawings and paintings, using a series of straight lines measured from the eye level of the viewer. The rules of perspective were defined by Filippo Brunelleschi around 1314. See also *aerial perspective*.

pigment - anything used to give colour to paints. Early pigments were made by grinding up naturally colourful rocks and metal ores; modern pigments are often made artificially.

plaster - a smooth, quick-drying paste, usually spread onto walls before painting.

Pointillism - a technique of painting in tiny dots of contrasting colours, developed by 19th-century French painter Georges Seurat.

Pompeii - an ancient *Roman* seaside town, not far from Naples, Italy, preserved by being buried under volcanic ash in the year 79.

Pop art - a type of art developed in the 1960s by artists including Andy Warhol and Roy Lichtenstein, drawing inspiration from the popular or "pop" imagery of advertisements and comic strips.

Pope - the leader of the *Catholic* Church, based in *Rome*.

portrait - a picture capturing a person's individual likeness, most often made of a living person.

precious stones - a name given to valuable gemstones or jewels.

Pre-Raphaelite Brotherhood - a group of 19th-century British painters, including John Everett Millais and William Holman Hunt, who felt art had lost its higher purpose ever since the time of the *Renaissance* painter Raphael. Inspired by *medieval* art, they painted *scenes* from the Bible, history and literature in *lifelike* detail and bright, jewel-like colours.

Protestant - a branch of the *Christian* Church originally set up by people protesting against the *Catholic* Church. People or countries that follow this faith are also known as Protestant.

Reformation - the time in the 16th century when a massive religious split between *Catholics* and *Protestants* divided Europe.

Renaissance - meaning "rebirth", it was the period around 500 years ago in Europe when people re-discovered ideas lost since *classical* times. It led to a revolution in European art and *culture*, and a craze for all things *classical*.

revolution - a dramatic change, or a sudden, violent uprising.

rococo - the name given to the delicate, elaborate art of 18th-century artists including Jean-Antoine Watteau.

Romans - an ancient people based in Italy, who conquered and ruled a vast empire around 2,000 years ago.

Rome - The capital city of Italy; also the capital city of the *Romans*.

saint - someone very holy, who is believed to have a special place in heaven.

scaffolding - a system of poles put up to help reach difficult places.

scene - the setting where something happens, or just a picture of something.

sculptor - someone who carves or models works of art from stone, clay or other materials. The works sculptors make are known as **sculptures** or **statues.**

self-portrait - a picture an artist makes of their own likeness.

signature - the artist's name, written by the artist on a painting to show who painted it.

sketch - a quick drawing or painting.

sketchbook - a book used for making quick drawings or paintings.

still life - a type of painting showing household objects such as tableware, flowers and fruit. Still life paintings were especially popular at the beginning of the 17th century, and were made by artists including Diego Velázquez and Rachel Ruysch.

Suprematist - a type of *abstract* art developed at the start of the 20th century by Russian artists including Kasimir Malevich, who thought their ideas were "supremely" important.

surreal - meaning "more than real", it was a type of art designed to be deliberately strange and disturbing, developed after the Second World War by artists including Salvador Dalí. The **Surrealists** painted dreamlike *scenes* of things that could never really happen, in a *lifelike* style. They wanted to explore ideas and feelings that weren't normally discussed.

Symbolists - a group of 19th-century artists, including Odilon Redon, who used symbols to express their ideas and feelings.

texture - the surface feel of anything.

vanishing point - the point at eye level in a *perspective* painting where parallel lines (lines that are the same distance apart all along their length) seem to merge in the distance.

Venus - the *Roman* goddess of love.

wanderyears - the time a *medieval* artist or craftworker spent travelling around, learning new skills.

watercolour - paint made by mixing *pigments* with water. Watercolour paint can be used in very thin, see-through layers.

workshop - a place where artists or craftworkers do their work.

Index

Acknowledgements

Every effort has been made to trace the copyright holders of the material in this book. If any rights have been omitted, the publishers offer their sincere apologies and will rectify this in any subsequent editions following notification. The publishers are grateful to the following organizations and individuals for their contributions and permission to reproduce material:

Cover: top, *The Creation of Adam* (1511-12) from the Sistine Chapel Ceiling (1508-12) by Michelangelo, fresco (post restoration), 280x570cm, Vatican Museums and Galleries, Vatican City, Italy/The Bridgeman Art Library; bottom middle, *Mona Lisa* (around 1503-6) by Leonardo, oil paint on wood, 77x53cm, © Gianni Dagli Orti/CORBIS; bottom left, *Impression: Sunrise, Le Havre* (1872) by Monet, oil paint on canvas, 48x63 cm, © Archivo Iconografico, S.A./CORBIS; cover artwork by Uwe Mayer and Ian McNee. **p1**: *Impression: Sunrise, Le Havre* (detail), see cover credit. **p2**: *January* (around 1413-16) from the *Les très riches heures du Duc de Berry* by the Limbourg Brothers, egg tempera paint on animal skin, 29x21cm, Ms 65/1284 f.1v/Musee Conde, Chantilly, France/Giraudon/The Bridgeman Art Library. **p6**: *Portrait of Terentius Neo and his wife* (detail) (around the year 50), fresco from Pompeii, Italy, 58x52 cm, © Araldo de Luca/CORBIS. **pp8-9**: *Bison* (around 19,000 years ago), cave painting from Lascaux, France, © C M Dixon/Ancient Art & Architecture Collection Ltd. **p11**: *Hunting in the marshes* (around 3,350 years ago) by an unknown artist, wall painting from Thebes, Egypt, 83x98cm, © Archivo Iconografico, S.A./CORBIS. **p12**: *Ladies in blue* (around 3,500 years ago), fresco from Crete, Greece, © Kevin Schafer/CORBIS. **p14**: see credit for p6. **p16**: *The Annunciation with St. Ansano and St. Margaret* (1333) by Martini (detail), egg tempera paint on wood, 263x305cm, © Summerfield Press/CORBIS. **p18**: *The Mother of God of Tenderness* (around 1131), egg tempera paint on wood, 75x53cm, photo © Scala, Florence/Trat'Jakov State Gallery, Moscow. **p21**: *St. Luke* (around 800), from the *Harley Golden Gospels*, egg tempera paint on animal skin, 37x25cm, © British Library Board, all rights reserved, Harley 2788. **p22**: see credit for p16. **p25**: see credit for p2. **p27**: *Bird studies* (before 1455) by Pisanello, watercolour paint on paper, Louvre, Paris, France/Lauros/Giraudon/The Bridgeman Art Library. **pp28-9**: *The Birth of Venus* (around 1485) by Botticelli (detail), egg tempera paint on canvas, 180x280cm, © Summerfield Press/CORBIS. **p31**: *The Arnolfini Portrait* (1434) by van Eyck, oil paint on wood, 84x57cm, © The National Gallery, London. **p32**: see credit for pp28-9. **pp34-5**: *Hunt in the Forest* (1436) by Uccello, oil paint on wood, 73x177cm, © Ashmolean Museum, University of Oxford, UK/The Bridgeman Art Library. **p37**: *Head of a Cherub* (around 1500-20) by Raphael, black chalk and charcoal on paper, 30x24cm, Hamburger Kunsthalle, Hamburg, Germany/The Bridgeman Art Library. **p38**: *The Holy Family* (about 1504-5) by Michelangelo, oil paint on wood, 120cm diameter, © Summerfield Press/CORBIS. **p40**: *Mona Lisa*, see cover credit. **p42**: *The Milkmaid* (about 1658-60) by Vermeer (detail), oil paint on canvas, 46x41cm, Rijksmuseum, Amsterdam, Holland/The Bridgeman Art Library. **p44**: *The Sacrifice of Isaac* (1603), by Caravaggio, oil paint on canvas, 104x135cm, Galleria degli Uffizi, Florence, Italy/Alinari/The Bridgeman Art Library. **p47**: *The Family of Philip IV* (around 1656) by Velázquez, oil paint on canvas, 316x276cm, Prado, Madrid, Spain/Giraudon/The Bridgeman Art Library. **p48**: see credit for p42. **p51**: *Still Life with Flowers* (before 1750) by Ruysch, oil paint on canvas, 95x80cm, Private Collection, Courtesy of Thomas Brod and Patrick Pilkington/The Bridgeman Art Library. **p52**: *Mr. and Mrs. Andrews* (1748-9) by Gainsborough, oil paint on canvas, 70x119cm, © The National Gallery, London. **pp54-5**: *The 'Fighting Temeraire' tugged to her Last Berth to be broken up, 1838* (1839) by Turner (detail), oil paint on canvas, 91x122cm, © The National Gallery, London. **p56**: *Execution of the Defenders of Madrid, 3rd May, 1808* (1818) by Goya, oil paint on canvas, 266x345cm, Prado, Madrid, Spain/The Bridgeman Art Library. **p58**: see credit for pp54-5. **p61**: *White Pegasus* (1908) by Redon, oil paint on canvas, 65x50cm, Private Collection/The Bridgeman Art Library. **p62**: *Impression: Sunrise, Le Havre*, see cover credit. **p65**: *Van Gogh's Bedroom at Arles* (1889) by van Gogh, oil paint on canvas, 73x91cm, Art Institute of Chicago, IL, USA/The Bridgeman Art Library. **p66**: *Suprematist Composition* (1915) by Malevich (detail), oil paint on canvas, 102x62cm, Stedelijk Museum, Amsterdam, The Netherlands/The Bridgeman Art Library. **p68**: *Mont Sainte-Victoire* (1902-4) by Cézanne, oil paint on canvas, 70x90cm, © Philadelphia Museum of Art/CORBIS. **p71**: see credit for p66. **p72**: *Travoys arriving with wounded at a dressing station, Smol, Macedonia, 1916* (1919) by Spencer, oil paint on canvas, © Imperial War Museum, London, UK/The Bridgeman Art Library. **pp74-5**: *Sheng-Tung* (1974) by Riley, acrylic paint on linen, 97x 229cm, photo © Christie's Images/CORBIS, artwork © Bridget Riley. **p76**: *Red Elvis* (1962) by Andy Warhol, screenprint, 175x132cm, image © Andy Warhol Foundation/CORBIS, artwork © The Andy Warhol Foundation for the Visual Arts/Corbis.

Edited by Rosie Dickins and Jane Chisholm. Art director: Mary Cartwright. Picture research by Ruth King. Digital imaging by John Russell and Nick Wakeford. With thanks to Hazel Maskell.